# Dotty Da Danger

# By
# Diane Ezzard

Book 3 in the Dotty Drinkwater
Mystery Series

## Other Books in the Series: -

**Dotty Dishes the Dirt - prequel**

1. Dotty Dices with Death
2. Dotty Dreads a Disaster
3. Dotty Dabbles in Danger
4. Dotty Discovers Diamonds
5. Dotty Deals with a Dilemma

## Other books by Diane Ezzard

The Sophie Brown mystery series –

**My Dark Decline – prequel**

1. I Know Your Every Move
2. As Sick As Our Secrets
3. The Sinister Gathering
4. Resentments and Revenge
5. A Life Lost
6. The Killing Cult

**Website:** http://dezzardwriter.com/
**Email:** support@dezzardwriter.com
**Facebook:** https://www.facebook.com/dezzardwriter/
**Twitter:** https://twitter.com/diane_ezzard
**Bookbub:** http://bit.ly/2OlnLE1
**Amazon:** https://amzn.to/2Qf2uZV

# Newsletter Sign-up

I hope you enjoy reading my novel as much as I enjoyed writing it. I am looking to build a relationship up with my readers, so occasionally I will be sending out newsletters. These will include otherwise untold information about the characters, things about myself, and other bits of news.

I would love you to join us and in return for giving me your email which will never be passed on to third parties, you will receive exciting offers and give-aways not found anywhere else.

You can find the sign-up page on my website

# Contents

| | |
|---|---|
| Other Books in the Series | 2 |
| Newsletter sign up | 5 |
| Novel | 7 |
| Reviews | 220 |
| VIP sign up reminder | 221 |
| About the author | 222 |
| Acknowledgements | 223 |
| Other books by the author | 224 |
| Bibliography | 241 |

# Chapter 1

"I've been looking forward to this all week." Dotty hitched her rucksack onto her shoulders.

"Thank goodness the rain that's been threatening stayed away." Rachel looked up at the sky and Kylie kicked a stone out of her path.

The sun shone, and the birds sang as the girls skipped down the lane, laughing and joking. What could possibly go wrong?

Dotty had organised her friends well. She brought along a homemade pastry-less cheese and onion quiche and some meat-free filo pastry sausage rolls especially for the recently turned veggie, Rachel. Kylie could pull her face all she wanted but it wouldn't deter the newly health-conscious Dotty who had also prepared a pasta and a rice salad. She had been battling to lose weight since the New Year and was now only a few pounds off reaching halfway to her goal. That would be a great achievement for Dotty. She yo-yoed with both her weight and the commitment to her plight. Rachel was supportive and liked to watch what she ate. She had made a Waldorf salad and a fruit salad. Kylie's contribution was crisps and nuts as well as the wine. She intended to bring ham sandwiches in protest at the rabbit food on offer but didn't wake up early enough to make them.

Kylie worked last night behind the bar at the Six Bells pub then went on to a nightclub with a few of the regulars who were having a birthday celebration. She was now suffering from the hangover from hell. Most folk would steer clear of booze after a heavy session but not Kylie. She intended to tackle it with more of the same. Hence the box of wine. This would be some picnic.

The path narrowed as the girls ventured forward through the endless pastures of green grass. Dotty glanced through the trees and saw cows stood in the meadow. That was a good sign. Hopefully, the weather would stay dry. A scarecrow stood valiantly in the middle of the field wearing old clothes looking almost human, its arms spread out wide.

"What is a scarecrow's favourite fruit?" Rachel asked, staring into the distance.

"I don't know, but I'm sure you're going to tell me." Kylie followed her friend's gaze.

"Straw-berries." Kylie groaned at Rachel's feeble attempt at a joke.

The light breeze caressed their bodies. Kylie's shorts had seen better days and the elastic waist wasn't performing as elastic should even with her ample frame. She kept stopping to heave them up and her body wriggled with the weight of her backpack. The wine got heavier by the minute but at least she had the satisfaction of knowing her load would be a lot lighter on the way home.

Dotty had brought along her poodle, Winnie and the dog tugged on her lead, itching to be free.

"Not until we get past Devil's Bridge Farm, Winnie. I don't want you scaring the sheep. Old Ned Bristow will be cross if you go near them again." Winnie was only a tiny animal, but with her eagerness, she was able to pull her owner faster than she would have liked. Dotty looked ahead. There was nothing but miles of soft green rolling hills, endless blue sky with a few fluffy white clouds dotted around, drifting slowly in the warm air. Birds flew overhead, and their chirping was drowned out by the girls' merry laughter. The sunshine improved everyone's mood.

"Are you looking forward to starting college in two weeks' time, Dotty?" Rachel asked.

"Oh, yes, and I'm so glad Kylie got on the same course as me."

"It will be tough fitting it around my job but working in the hair and beauty field has always been something I've wanted to do. When you signed up, Dotty it was the motivation I needed to commit myself to a proper career." Kylie walked on the grass to avoid a muddy patch.

"I'm the same. I'm glad I've found something I'm really interested in. You won't be on your own working to pay your way through college though, Kylie. My dad only agreed to me doing the course if I cough up for my keep. I start working at the wine bar next Friday."

"It won't feel like work at that trendy place. They get lots of celebs in there. We'll be jealous, won't we, Kylie?" Rachel hopped over a large boulder.

"Yeah, you won't have grumpy Ned Bristow and his cronies propping up the bar moaning about the state of the economy or whatever else they grumble about."

"You must both pop down and see me, and bring Harry, Rachel. The manager told me that the staff aren't allowed to ask for autographs if someone famous comes in as it doesn't look professional." Dotty laughed. "If someone in the public eye arrives, I'll tip you guys the wink and you can call in for a selfie with them."

"Good idea. I've always fancied having my bedroom wall filled with photos of me hanging out with Gary Barlow or the rest of Take That." Kylie breathed heavily. The rucksack pulled on her shoulders.

"You'll be lucky to see those guys, but I hear Katie Price and a few of the EastEnders mob get in."

"Listen, I'll settle for Ken Dodd, I don't mind." A butterfly fluttered in front of Rachel's nose.

"I think he's dead, isn't he?" Dotty looked across at Rachel.

"Yes, it'll be a miracle if you spot him." Kylie laughed.

"I could make a few quid with that photo then." Dotty giggled and the other two joined in.

Dotty breathed in the fresh smell of recently mown grass as they walked towards a small bridge. The three girls and Winnie trotted over it, looking down at the sparkling cool stream below.

Suddenly, the girls heard a loud rumbling noise. Dotty, who was now at the front of the pack with Winnie, stopped in her tracks. The little dog barked. She turned to the others, frowning.

"What is that noise?" she asked. Kylie shrugged her shoulders.

"Search me." They all stood looking around as if a spaceship was about to land.

"It's coming from the field over there." Rachel pointed ahead and to the right. Unable to allay their curiosity, the friends went over to the hedge to investigate.

"It sounds like thunder." Rachel looked around, puzzled. Kylie's eyes moved skywards. Her arms flew in the air.

"It's over at Devil's Bridge Farm." Dotty shielded her eyes with her hand to protect them from the glare of the sun and peered across.

"That's right, gosh. Look at that, the cattle are stampeding. I didn't realise cows did things like that." Dotty watched in the distance as the animals rushed across the meadow. Dust and smoke puffed up in their wake. Kylie raised her eyebrows.

"Maybe that's what they do when it's lunchtime and they're starving. That's how I feel. Come on, girls let's get a move on. My belly is rumbling almost as loud as those beasts."

The girls may have been shocked at what they saw but it didn't deter them from their quest to find a suitable spot to set down their picnic.

They walked on past a meadow filled with wild poppies. Dotty was in awe of the beauty of the scenery. She had suggested to her policeman friend, Dave, that they come and do some painting out here. She would mention it again next time they spoke as they both had a keen interest and talent for art.

The heat got to Kylie. She stopped and leant against a tree. Her face looked flushed. She took the rucksack off her shoulders and massaged the small hollow in her back whilst extending her body.

"Do you want a breather?" Dotty asked. She nodded, so they waited for a few moments until she got her energy back. Winnie barked, keen to continue. She hadn't spotted any rabbits yet. They carried on along the perimeter of the farmland. Dotty spotted two large container lorries leaving the premises and driving down the lane in the distance. She thought no more about it as she turned her focus to the sounds of nature around her. Birds chirped in the trees. Onward they went. They turned a corner. Some way further up the path, Rachel stopped.

"How about here?" she asked. She glanced at the others for approval. Her long blonde hair had been braided, and she looked the coolest of the three wearing a sun hat and a thin cotton blue dress and trainers.

"It's as good a spot as any for a picnic by the river. What do you think, Dotty?"

"Fine by me." As she spoke, Dotty undid her bag and started unfolding the tartan throw for them to sit on.

"Good, 'cos I'm spitting feathers. All this walking has made me thirsty." Kylie delved into her rucksack and took out the box of wine to open before anyone changed their minds. She poured drinks into three plastic cups and gave them out to her friends. Dotty opened her plastic containers and set them out in a row for everyone to dive in. She wafted a fly away.

"Come on girls, help yourselves before these pesky flies eat everything."

"What a great idea this was, coming for a picnic. Harry will be so jealous. He sulked earlier because he wanted me to go with him to see his nana. I told him this was pre-arranged, and I couldn't let you down."

"Good for you, Rachel. If there's anything left over, we can save him a doggy bag." Kylie laughed, doubting there would be any remains. Kylie loved her food and usually devoured everything put in front of her. Her eating habits weren't the most attractive as she salivated over the various savoury delights.

"I won't be dieting this week," she said. "My male fan club will have to put up with a bit of meat on my bones." She shimmied then sat on the rug. The nearest she got to a steady boyfriend like Rachel was her married lover, Kenny. She only saw him sporadically so made up for his lack of attention by seeing her old flame, Barry on the side. Dotty had been single for some time. She didn't have the greatest track record when it came to men. She recently had a crush on Dave the policeman, until she found out he was gay. Now they were the best of friends.

They finished their food and Dotty removed her shoes and went for a closer look at the river. A white feather floated down in front of her nose. That was supposed to be a good sign — it wasn't. The soft earth cushioned her step as she made her way to the water's edge. Winnie joined her. Dotty splashed her feet in the water and Winnie followed suit. It was icy cold. Spotting some fish, she moved in to get a better view. There were stepping-stones to walk across, so she stood on one. It was very slippery. Putting her arms out to steady herself, she gingerly moved onto the next stone. That was equally as slimy, and she became unsteady.

"Whoa, it's a bit dodgy here. Anyone else coming for a look?" As she spoke, she struggled with her centre of gravity. She held out her arms to balance. Unable to stand up straight, she lost her footing and went headfirst into the cool crisp water.

"Aargh!" she cried as she fell into the river, splashing away. Her friends had been watching from the embankment and came running over. They couldn't contain themselves and laughed out loud. Dotty's long auburn hair dripped forward over her face. Thankfully, the water was only shallow, so Dotty could clamber out. She looked like a drowned rat. Her hair was ruined, and she was soaked.

"Oh, Dotty." Kylie sniggered.

"What a catastrophe. Neither of you came to save me." Dotty took off her shorts and t-shirt and put them on a tree branch to dry. Her modesty wouldn't allow her to remove any more. Hopefully, with the sun beating down, it should have her things dry in no time.

"We were too busy laughing." Rachel smiled.

"I'm such an idiot." Dotty sighed.

By the time they were ready to leave, her clothes were only slightly damp. She had no choice but to dress. They packed up their belongings. Kylie had drunk the lion's share of the wine, so became very chatty, harbouring on about anything and everything. Her cheeks glowed from too much sun and alcohol. The three girls and Winnie crossed the meadow towards the main path. As they did so, Dotty spotted a sign in the field.

"I better check what that sign says. I wouldn't like us to be trespassing. Here, can you take Winnie's lead for a moment?" She clomped across the muddy terrain while Winnie and the others waited. Worried that they were on private land, she traversed the muddy terrain to read the notice. Underfoot became boggy, and she started sinking. She screamed out, trying to keep her touch light. As her feet sank into the mire, she tried to compensate by raising her legs out as high as possible. She looked like she was dancing in a field of hot potatoes. As she touched the surface with each footstep, she heard a squelching sound which took her feet deeper into the mud. Unfortunately, her shoes didn't survive the escapade. Her feet came out of them as she hopped and jumped to safety. Dotty watched incredulously as her shoes disappeared sinking into the ground. They had gone — drowned in a sea of mud. She took a stick and began prodding the surface to feel for her brown leather flat shoes. Even though she poked around the earth hoping to retrieve them, they were nowhere to be seen.

"Are you okay, Dotty?" Rachel called from the other side of the meadow.

"I've lost my shoes," she cried. By now, Dotty's legs were caked in dark brown mud. By the time she joined the others, her feet and legs were a smelly muddy sight.

"Oh, Dotty, what a mess you look." Rachel stared at her pitiful barefooted friend, holding her nose. "What are you going to do? Here, put these plastic bags on your feet." Rachel helped Dotty by tying the plastic around her ankles. She looked like the sad scarecrow now, but Rachel said nothing. As they made their way back along the main road, Kylie had a thought.

"Did you find out what the sign said, Dotty?"

"You won't believe it."

"Why? What did it say?" Rachel asked.

"It said — beware of sinking mud."

Poor Dotty hadn't had the best of days. It was still muddy underfoot from the recent rain. When they reached a section of the path full of puddles, Kylie picked her up and gave her a piggy-back. It was surprising they didn't both fall over, given the amount Kylie had drunk.

As they walked back along the trail towards Devil's Bridge Farm, the girls noticed a lot of police activity. Something big was going down. Too curious to walk straight past, the girls hovered around the entrance to the farm. A uniformed police officer stood on guard. He sniggered when Dotty walked up to him. She ignored his response to her attire.

"What's going on?" she asked him. Winnie barked.

"Someone's been trampled to death."

"You're joking. Is it someone who lives at the farm?"

"Sorry, we don't know. Now, move along. I've got to keep the area clear."

## Chapter 2

The incident at the farm had gotten the villagers talking but Dotty had largely stayed out of the speculation. A few days later, she was at home organising what she needed to do to get ready for her new college course. She glanced out of the window. The weather had taken a turn for the worse. Dark clouds loomed overhead. She checked the time. Hopefully, she could nip to the chemist's before the rain came. Her legs needed their monthly depilation. It would be criminal to show her hairy legs to the world, especially in front of her new fellow students. She had to make a good first impression. She had already invested in some new makeup and had experimented on her look. Dotty always took pride in her appearance. She never veered too far from the fifties look she so admired, and her new purple eyeliner looked the business. Her hair had been trimmed and her nails manicured. Now it was just the finishing touches, having her eyebrows waxed and making sure the rest of her skin was smooth and hair-free. It was high-maintenance work looking good, but she felt it was necessary. Kylie went even further with her false nails and tan, but then she had more available income to throw on her beauty regime than Dotty.

She popped on her green Barbour jacket and tied her silk Liberty scarf around her neck. Even going to the local shops, she kept up her standards. As she applied a final coat of lipstick, she glanced in the mirror. It would be good to bump into Mr Right now. Instead, the only person she saw was her neighbour from across the road, Betty Simpson.

"Are you ready to start college?" Betty asked as she bent over dead heading her roses. She winced as she straightened her back and looked over at Dotty. Betty's gardening gear comprised a dark blue gaberdine coat that covered her knees, together with a grey floppy velour hat. She wore bright-green gardening gloves.

"Just a few last-minute things to do, Betty." Dotty didn't want to go into detail about her underarm exfoliating routine or anything else for that matter.

"Your mum tells me she lent you some money to buy the equipment you need. I hope you get your use out of it this time and it's not another birdbrain idea of yours that only lasts five minutes."

Dotty didn't know whether to be sore with her mum or Betty for that remark. Sometimes. Betty's blunt manner stung. She had a knack of being tactless. Her harsh criticism didn't go down well. In reality, Dotty was heading towards thirty and still hadn't decided what to do with her life. Her dad had been upset that she never followed his footsteps and joined the police force. Dotty hoped she had now found something she wanted to do. She had tried various occupations from chocolate making to gardening as well as being a croupier and a saleswoman. Her worst job so far was working in a sausage factory. Nothing could be more horrific than that. She hoped that her love of hair and makeup had set her on the right path to a future career she could enjoy.

"It wasn't cheap to get everything on the list, so Mum helped out. I hope I can make a success of this." Dotty's face looked sad as her mouth turned down at the edges. Betty hadn't noticed that her comments may have wounded Dotty.

"Well, good luck, dear." Betty patted Dotty's arm.

"Is there any news on the mystery man trampled to death at Devil's Bridge Farm?" If Betty Simpson didn't know, then it was unlikely anyone else did. Betty folded her arms across her chest.

"No, no one seems to know him, by all accounts. Has your dad heard anything, him being an ex-bobby?"

"No, and Ned Bristow said he had never met the man."

"That seems strange, don't you think?"

"Ramblers walk along that route, so maybe not."

"Surely, someone must have missed him and reported his disappearance by now. I mean, it's been a few days." Betty waved to the postman across the road. "Nothing for me, today, Pat?" The Irish postman preferred to be called Paddy, but Betty took great delight in nicknaming him Postman Pat.

"No, Betty, not today."

"That's good. It means no bills." She winked at Dotty then turned back towards Paddy. "Have you heard anything about the poor man who was killed at Ned's place by those mad cows?" she shouted.

"As soon as I hear anything, I'll let you know, to be sure, Betty."

"Okay, Pat. Top of the morning to you." Betty tried to imitate an Irish accent, but it sounded more like Indian. Paddy waved as he continued his route. Betty moved in closer towards Dotty. "It's not right, letting dangerous beasts loose on the public like that. I wouldn't trust old Farmer Bristow as far as I could throw him," she whispered. Dotty went into one of her daydreams. She had a picture in her head of Betty throwing the large farmer by his feet. They could start up a competition, like tossing the caber in Scotland only here in rural Sussex it would be slinging the farmer across the field. She imagined Betty standing on a podium receiving a gold medal at the Olympics for throwing a farmer the furthest. "Are you listening to me, Dotty?"

"What was that, Betty?" Dotty shook her head and blinked.

"There's been a whisper about strange goings-on at his farm."

"Really, like what?"

"I don't know but mark my words, I'll be keeping my nose to the ground."

Dotty didn't have the heart to tell Betty it should be her ear. She now pictured Betty sliding along the pavement like a pig snorting truffles with her hand cupped over her nose sniffing out to find out what might be happening.

"I wouldn't expect anything else from you, Betty." Betty frowned, not sure how to take that comment.

"I hear the poor blighter had to be airlifted to hospital but never regained consciousness. Old Ned won't be happy. It will mean the Health and Safety Executive will be snooping around his place, not to mention the police. He'll have to be on his best behaviour." Betty laughed. "He'll find that hard. If he was doing anything illegal, he will have to make the place squeaky clean." Her comments jolted Dotty's memory. She and her friends realised that when they heard and spotted cattle stampeding, that was probably when the accident happened. She recalled that not long after they heard the rumbling of the cattle on that fateful day, they spotted two large container-like juggernaut lorries leaving the premises. She wondered if that had any relevance. Could there be any truth in Betty's words? "They took him to St. George's in London. They must have better facilities there." Betty shook her head. "This will wake up the community. Once the inquest is over, mark my words, the locals will be up in arms. If they think those cows aren't safe, they'll want action. We can't have mad agitated cattle grazing in our midst. You and Winnie could be in danger. I wonder if something spooked them to make them behave like that. He'll have to put signs up now saying it's not safe to enter the common. He won't be pleased having to spend any money. I reckon they'll make him move his cows to another field away from the public footpath. There's been a wave of shock around the village. Everyone is talking about it."

"Yeah, my friend, Kylie has been researching cows that go berserk. You know how she likes to google things to find out information. Apparently, it isn't an isolated incident. Cattle attack people more than you realise and about a quarter of those attacks are fatal."

"So, what causes them to do that?"

"Sometimes, its cows with calves protecting their young. Dogs can cause cattle to become aggressive. Certain continental breeds are known for being more highly strung. I'm not sure what breed Farmer Bristow has."

"If he's breeding mad cows, then something needs to be done about it."

"I thought it was dogs he bred?"

"Oh, he's got his fingers in more than one pie. But that man is skating on thin ice and will need to watch his step among the locals. It's a good job no one knows who the poor victim was. If it had been a resident, the locals would lynch Old Ned."

Dotty nodded at the grim idea of the farmer being strung up to a tree. She shuddered.

# Chapter 3

Dotty set her alarm early to give herself extra time to get ready. She wanted to look her best for her first day at college. She imagined most of the students would be fresh out of school. Probably, only she and Kylie would be getting on in years, now they were closer to thirty. She showered, and blow-dried her hair, popping rollers in for extra bounce. Her make up needed to be flawless today. It was likely to be scrutinised by the others as she would do with them. She toyed with the idea of wearing false lashes like Kylie always did but, in the end, settled for her new purple eyeliner.

The girls had got together the previous week for a uniform-trying-on day. Rachel came along to pass comment.

"You could do with a couple of darts in your beauty outfit. That lilac shade isn't as flattering as the black hairdressing tunic."

Dotty twirled from side to side as she checked her body.

"Yes, you're right. Pass me that sewing box, Kylie, I'll stick a few pins in."

"Can you alter mine while you're at it?" Kylie asked. "I feel like a sack of potatoes in this." Dotty knew that no amount of darts would make her friend look thinner. They got changed out of their outfits while Dotty whipped out her sewing machine. She had their outfits turned into more figure-hugging creations in no time. She and Kylie did a final fitting.

"You both look great, girls. You will do a brilliant job at college. I can feel it in my bones." They hugged.

"Thanks, Rachel and even if we don't, I'll make sure we enjoy ourselves." Kylie winked at her friend.

"So, if someone comes in and asks you for a bob, only longer, will you give them a Robert?" Rachel grinned and Dotty shook her head. She was used to Rachel's dumb jokes now. The three of them had been inseparable since senior school when they got a detention for being in one of the classrooms when they weren't supposed to be. Dotty remembered having to write an essay on why it was important to follow instructions. She had a flashback to that day as she swept her maroon-coloured tortoiseshell clips in the sides of her hair. She hoped college wouldn't be strict like that. Her stomach churned, filled with both excitement and reservation. She hadn't made a success of much in her life so far and she worried she wouldn't make the grade again. It was hard playing second fiddle to her brother, Joe all the time. He had always been the brainy one in the family whereas she seemed to fall short at everything.

Today, she wore her navy and white spotty fifties style dress with the tucked in waist. Her new eyeliner and deep red lipstick complimented the look. She turned and checked her appearance in the full-length mirror. Happy with her efforts, she popped into the kitchen and drained the last of her coffee. Her dad sat reading the newspaper behind a plate of crumbs. That was all that remained of the jam and toast he greedily consumed a few minutes earlier. He would need that sustenance for a round of golf with his pal, Ray later.

"Good luck on your first day. I hope it goes well." The sound of her dad's voice came from behind the paper. Dotty raised her eyebrows in astonishment.

"Thanks, Dad." Dotty believed that since she turned down the opportunity to join the police, her dad wasn't interested in her career. He never spoke about her with affection, the way he did with Joe. Joe had recently moved into the halls of residence in Manchester to do a degree in computer science. Her mum had been upset that he moved so far away, but Dotty saw it as an opportunity. She heard that nights out up north were legendary, so she planned to visit him to check out the nightlife once he settled in.

This was the only time her dad had acknowledged her starting college other than when she told her parents she had enrolled and been successful in gaining a place. On that occasion, he commented that she still needed to pay for her keep — very encouraging. It may not be university, but her mum seemed pleased for her. With her dad, however, Dotty saw the disappointment in his eyes, and it choked her up. Getting this positive statement from him now was a big deal. Dotty breathed a heavy sigh. She pulled on her leather jacket and picked up her bag.

"Bye, Dad."

"Have a good day."

"You too." As she closed the front door behind her, she looked across the road. Betty Simpson stood there with two of her friends, Audrey and Gladys. They started clapping.

"Go on, Dotty, let them have it."

"Good luck, dear," they shouted over.

"What are you lot doing there?"

"We're here to give you a good send-off. We've watched you grow and blossom. You'll make your parents proud."

"Thank you, ladies. It means a lot."

Dotty blinked back a tear. She couldn't believe it. Betty could be an absolute nightmare of a woman with her interfering ways at times, but she proved here that deep down she did have a heart. She and her friends had stood and clapped her on her first day at school. They did it again when she proudly showed off her new uniform at the start of senior school and now this.

She waved across at them then got into her car. She shook her head as she drove up the road. People could still surprise her in a positive way. Betty would be back to moaning about her again by tomorrow but for today, Dotty could revel in that glimpse of Betty's caring side.

She didn't have to be there until 10 o'clock and had arranged to pick Kylie up on the way. Kylie didn't drive. She failed her theory test twice and had given up on the idea for now. She was happy to be chauffeured around by friends. Dotty pulled up outside Kylie's flat and beeped her horn. Her friend came to the window and waved. This was a big day for them both. Neither girl had been blessed with an academic brain, so they both had reservations about their ability to succeed. Kylie opened the passenger door and threw her bag in the back. Dotty turned the music down, so they could chat.

"Did you get all the items on the starter pack list?" she asked her friend.

"They were out of stock of the largest size rollers and I couldn't get hold of a blackhead extractor. How about you?"

"The blackhead extractor is the only thing I'm missing. I tried all the wholesalers on the list."

"Oh dear, we could have a crisis on our hands. Imagine it, front-page news. What if all this air pollution has created a national blackhead epidemic and there aren't enough tools being manufactured to cope with the demand?" Kylie laughed.

"Yes, it could start a war of women scrapping to get their skin looking good." Dotty giggled.

"After speaking to Milly who did the course a few years ago, you end up losing half your stuff, anyway. People borrow each other's things and forget to give them back."

"My gran paid for my kit. She will go berserk if I lose anything. I must put my name on all my gear."

"We should colour code everything, you know, like they do with sheep."

"That's not such a bad idea." The girls drove on in silence for a few minutes. Thoughts of sheep got Dotty thinking.

"Have you heard if they've discovered who that poor man was who died up at Devils Bridge Farm yet?"

"No, from what I've heard there are no reports of any missing persons in the area."

"He was in his forties, wasn't he?"

"That's right, but it's a complete mystery. He must have loved ones somewhere who are concerned about him."

Dotty nodded and pulled into the college car park.

## Chapter 4

Kylie's short platinum blonde hair made her easily recognisable as they stood in the hall. This week she had dyed the front a lilac shade to match her beauty tunic. Dotty stood weighing up the others. Some of the girls looked stunning, which did nothing to ease Dotty's insecurity. Not everyone looked so glamorous though. The students were asked to do an ice-breaking exercise to mingle. Dotty got lumbered with a girl called Rose who didn't look like she'd put a comb through her hair. She had obviously tried to curl it, but it looked more dishevelled than curly. Plus, she wore blusher that was totally in the wrong place on her cheeks. She hadn't sucked in when she applied it. The poor girl just didn't look right. She looked more like an unkempt Father Christmas without the beard. Dotty wondered how Rose would fit in with some of these girls who almost passed for models. Next, they sat and listened to a speech from the Head. The girl sat to Dotty's right whispered in her ear.

"What do you think?"

Dotty wasn't too sure what she meant. What did she think about what — the tutor, the speech, the course, the other students, maybe? With a shrug of her shoulders, she gazed at the strawberry-blonde haired stunner and gulped.

"Well, it's early days." The young woman looked at Dotty and smiled. That answer must have sufficed.

"I'm Becky." She held her hand out to shake Dotty's but when Dotty glanced towards the front, she noticed the tutor looked straight at her, so she didn't respond. She waited a few moments until the principal started talking again.

"You are young people embarking on an exciting future together...."

"Hi, I'm Dotty Drinkwater," Dotty whispered, holding her right hand out towards Becky, whilst keeping one eye on the front of the hall. Becky shook it vigorously.

"I wish she'd shut up, so we could get to know each other properly," Becky said out loud. A few students turned and glared at her. After the initial speech ended, the room of students was split into two groups. Names were called out and Dotty waited, hoping to be with Kylie. Sadly, it was not meant to be, and she was allocated to the other group. Dotty was stuck with Rose, who looked like a square peg in a round hole, and noisy Becky. Neither seemed like the in-crowd. Dotty wondered if she would fit in.

She sat with Becky for the first lecture which was the boring stuff about health and safety. Becky made her feelings known by sighing loudly every few seconds. At the break time, Dotty couldn't wait to get away from her and she excused herself to find Kylie. She sent her friend a text and they arranged to meet in the refectory. Another message pinged through as she rushed along the corridor. She looked down to check it, so she wasn't watching where she was going. She didn't notice the young man coming from the other direction. They collided, and the young guy dropped his bag and the books he was carrying.

"I'm so sorry, here let me." Dotty bent to pick up the books and files.

"It's fine. It's not a problem." As they both went to grab the same book, the cover tore.

"Oh no, I'm such a clumsy oaf." Dotty looked at the damage, in horror. The poor student looked flustered. "Please, let me help. I can sort it." Dotty noticed how shiny his brown brogue shoes were.

They were still crouched on the floor as their eyes met. She thought she had never seen a more handsome guy. The alluring aroma of his heady aftershave wafted underneath her nostrils. With his brown eyes and tanned complexion, he looked like an Adonis. She wondered if he was foreign. His black hair was neatly gelled. As she tore her eyes away from his, she noticed his perfectly manicured fingers and expensive-looking watch. In Dotty's eyes, this young dreamboat in front of her was the most perfect specimen of a man she had ever seen.

"Please, allow me to treat you to a coffee," Dotty said. "It's the least I can do for the mess I've caused.

"No, it's okay, honestly." They both stood up simultaneously as Kylie turned the corner and bumped into them both.

"What's all this then?"

"Oh, we stumbled into each other." The young man brushed his trousers. Dotty noticed how neatly pressed they were.

"So, have you been introduced to my classmate, James?"

"No, I'm Dotty, pleased to meet you."

"And I'm James Bristow, likewise." They shook hands and Dotty thought how like Kylie it was to get her hands on this hottie first. After the introductions, the three of them walked down to buy drinks. They sat together at the far side of the room and Kylie leaned over to Dotty, wasting no time filling her in.

"James lives in one of those new penthouse apartments up by North Road."

"Oh, wow, lucky you. That must have set you back a pretty penny." Dotty looked longingly into his eyes.

"Yes, they're not cheap but I'm fortunate. I've done alright for myself. I have a rich boyfriend." Dotty's smile disappeared. She didn't want to show her disappointment in this turn of events, so tried to bring back up the corners of her mouth. This was the story of her life. All the best-looking guys were unavailable. It was a good job she found out now before she made a fool of herself like she nearly did with her policeman friend, Dave.

"So, what does your boyfriend do for a living, if he's rich?" Kylie felt relaxed enough around James to ask personal questions. He had a warmth about him that was endearing. His eyes crinkled at the corner when he smiled.

"You wouldn't believe me if I told you."

"Go on, try us." Kylie nudged his arm. James laughed.

"He's a prince."

"Get away with you. You're having us on." Dotty scrunched up her nose.

"I told you, you wouldn't believe me."

"A prince, as in royalty?" Dotty's eyes widened.

"That's right."

"So, where did you meet him then?"

"In a nightclub. I knew he must have been a celebrity or something when I first saw him because he had a whole area sectioned off for him and his entourage. That alone must have set him back an arm and a leg. He invited me and two of my friends to join him. It was love at first sight for both of us. The following week, he flew me to Paris in his private jet and ever since I've been living off champagne and caviar. We had a whirlwind courtship and moved in together after three weeks."

"Oo, lucky you. What an amazing story. Why can't I meet someone like him? I end up with the local plumber." Kylie raised her chin and eyebrows.

"At least a plumber comes in handy. At least you get your boiler serviced. I only meet idiots and they never have two halfpennies to rub together." Dotty shook her head.

"I get more than my boiler serviced don't you worry." Kylie winked and James laughed. He was enjoying getting to know his two new friends.

"So, why are you on this course?" Dotty asked. "I wouldn't have thought you'd need to work with a partner like that."

"For my self-esteem and I love hair and makeup. My life hasn't always been easy, growing up on a farm. I love animals but I didn't enjoy the mucking out and getting my hands dirty. I've never been good around mud unless it's a face pack." James patted his face and looked at his clean fingernails. "You may know my father."

"Why, who is your dad?"

"Ned Bristow."

"You're joking." Kylie's eyebrows were raised. "As in Farmer Bristow?"

"The very same."

"Well, I'll be darned. What a small world. You don't look alike."

"No, I get my good looks from my mother's side," James said placing his hand under his chin.

"I can't believe it," Dotty said.

"Unfortunately, it's true."

"Unfortunately?" Kylie queried.

"Would you want a father like him, brash and full of himself? He's selfish to the core and doesn't give two hoots about anyone but himself." Kylie thought for a moment. She was used to seeing the farmer's raucous ways along with his temper when he came into the pub every weekend. The way James spoke about him, she thought there was more to their family history.

"Probably not, no," she replied, honestly. She stared at James wondering how this wonderful-looking specimen of a man could have been produced by Ned Bristow.

## Chapter 5

"The tragedy that happened at your dad's farm was awful, wasn't it?" Dotty cocked her head as she looked across at James. The sadness in his eyes went deep into the recesses of his soul.

"I don't know much about it." His head turned away.

"Oh, really? I'd have thought your dad would be talking about it all the time."

"He may be, but I haven't spoken to him on the subject."

"You do surprise me." James looked pensive. He thought for a moment before continuing.

"It's not just that subject I haven't spoken to him about. My father and I don't speak. I haven't seen him for over five years."

"Oh, how sad. That can't be easy for you." Dotty watched James's expression. The steely hardness in his eyes was apparent. She figured that was for the world to see. The tell-tale sign that he had been affected by the split was when his chin quivered. James averted his eyes as he contemplated how much to reveal to his new friends. The silence that ensued was broken when Kylie touched his hand and gave him a soft smile.

"We're here for you if you ever want to discuss it."

"Thank you. That means a lot." His eyes glazed over, and he sighed heavily.

"What about your mum? Do you see her?" Dotty asked.

"Yes, we meet up regularly. My mother has accepted me for who I am, but she won't go against my father. I am no longer welcome at the farm, the home where I grew up."

"That's terrible, James. I don't know how you cope with being estranged." For Dotty, her family was everything. That was one reason she still lived at home. She couldn't bear to be apart from her mum and dad. James' words touched a nerve though because she did so much over the years to try to please her dad and she knew how difficult that had been. In her eyes, she never came up to the mark.

James took in a deep breath. His lungs filled with air and he whistled through his teeth and nodded.

"I might as well tell you what happened." He swallowed. "I realised I was different in my teens. I mean, there were probably earlier signs such as wanting to play with dolls, but when you live on a farm, you have to muck in and become butch. Queens aren't renowned for swilling out pigs and helping with calving, but I just got on with it. I enjoyed being around animals. Some of the jobs were gross though. I hated how dirty the work was, which sounds stupid coming from a farmer's son. I had my first homosexual experience at school. I had a crush on Gavin. He was a good-looking boy and all the girls fancied him. I developed strong feelings for him. We became good friends, and I had my suspicions he was like me, but I couldn't be sure. No one spoke about such things back then. Our first encounter was classic, behind the bike sheds." James laughed.

"We kept our relationship secret, but it tore me apart. I fell in love with him and wanted the world to know. He lit up my life, but nobody ever knew. It felt like I was living a double life. I reckon I could easily get a job as a spy with everything I've been through, all the deception and secrecy. We split up not long after leaving school. We both went to different universities. I became insecure being away from him and he couldn't cope with my neediness and jealousy. By then, I was in Exeter, doing a degree in husbandry. I found a girlfriend, Sarah. It was my way of coping with Gavin's rejection. I rebelled against my sexuality. It was also because my mother kept going on at me to find a nice girl, you know the sort of thing she'd say. When are you going to settle down and get yourself a lovely girlfriend and when will you make me a grandma?" He acted out his mum's voice as he spoke.

"It cut me up every time she asked, so I started seeing Sarah, but things didn't work out. We went out for a while but there was no physical side to the relationship. It was only to show the world I was a so-called normal human being." James highlighted those words with speech marks in the air. "Secretly, I had started going to gay bars and enjoying myself but leading a double life was difficult. I met a guy called Charles. All his family knew he was gay, so, eventually, I plucked up the courage to come out. I was in my final year at uni, and it was a tough time with exams and everything." James wiped a tear from the corner of his eye. Dotty passed him a tissue.

"So, what happened, James?" Kylie's hands were clasped together like she was praying.

"It was two weeks before my birthday. My mother badgered me to bring my imaginary girlfriend home. I hadn't told my parents that Sarah and I were history, you see. Mother had been going on, asking if we were getting engaged and all that nonsense. I knew it was time to tell them the truth. I came home from uni that weekend. It had been some time since I'd visited. Distancing myself from them seemed like the easiest option to cope with my lies. I told them I had something important to tell them, so I wanted them both to be there. Now, with hindsight, I realise that my mother expected me to say I was getting married to Sarah, and that was what she had built herself up to hear. So, when I told her I was gay, she fainted."

Kylie put her hand over her mouth and gasped.

"How terrible," Dotty said.

"That wasn't the worse reaction. The bombshell came from my father. He was raging. He told me I was no son of his. As far as he was concerned, I no longer existed. I was not welcome in their home. He said if I didn't come to my senses and sort myself out, he wanted nothing more to do with me. There was one point that I thought he was going to hit me because he was so angry. He asked if there was somewhere that I could go and get help."

"How did you feel, getting that reaction?" Dotty asked.

"Gutted, of course. I mean, it wasn't the best response I had hoped for. It couldn't have been much worse. Part of me was relieved that it was out in the open. I had lived a lie for years and once my parents knew, it meant I was free to tell everyone, free to be who I was destined to be. I no longer had to keep up this wall of pretence. It took a lot of courage but by coming out, I can finally be the real me."

"That must have taken an immense amount of bravery on your part, James." Dotty's eyes looked sad. He nodded.

"And haven't you spoken to your father since?" Kylie asked.

"No, the bigoted old man can rot in hell as far as I'm concerned. He has been true to his word and hasn't welcomed me back home. I didn't finish my degree after that. Their reaction caused me to go into a downward spiral. I drank heavily and used drugs at the time. I felt alone. It was my gay friends who pulled me out from the depths of despair. I lived in London back then. Ironically, I only came back to Sussex when I met Khalid and we moved in together. It may be rubbing my father's nose in, being so close to him now, but Father is the one with the problem, not me."

"So, do you still see your mum?" Kylie asked.

"Yes, we meet for coffee once a week and a meal once a month. She has met Khalid and likes him. Now that she has come to terms with my sexuality, I think she is happy for me. At least, that's what I'd like to believe. I doubt that my father will ever change his views, but now, I am here doing what I want to do with my life, and I intend to enjoy myself."

"Good for you and thank you for sharing that with us, James. You're inspirational." Dotty smiled.

"Be careful, any compliments are likely to go to my head and I'm unbearable when I'm big-headed." They all laughed.

## Chapter 6

College life proved to be everything Dotty and Kylie hoped for. They settled in well and couldn't wait to tell their friend, Rachel, when they met up for their weekly rendezvous at the Strawberry Tea rooms. The pink and white décor was very welcoming. It highlighted the cleanliness of the café and the aromas coming from the fresh coffee and culinary delights made the girls swoon. Kylie chose a large slice of coffee and walnut cake to go with her cappuccino. She picked up the dainty fork, turned it over, then put it down and picked the piece of cake up in her hand and took a bite. Coffee buttercream oozed out the side and she scooped it up and licked her lips.

"This is better than any orgasm." She smiled. Rachel and Dotty looked at each other.

"Is everything okay between you and Kenny?"

"Kenny?" Kylie looked shocked. "Who's Kenny? I haven't seen him in ages. When his son started playing truant from school, he wasn't very attentive towards me. He started spending more time with his wife and kids, sadly. I always knew the relationship didn't have any legs, and I got sick of feeling neglected. No, I've moved on from him. I did meet a new guy in the pub last week, but I won't be seeing him again. He wasn't one of our regulars, but we had a bit of banter and he came back to my place."

"What was his name?"

"Frank and the reason I didn't tell you about him before now was because he's already history."

"Oh dear, why is that then?" Dotty asked.

"His performance wasn't up to scratch."

"His performance?" Rachel had been slurping from a straw of homemade lemonade. She put the glass on the table.

"Yeah, if he's no good in the sack, he doesn't get a second date."

"I see."

"Not only was he a rubbish lover, but he was scared of mice."

"Scared of mice," Rachel repeated. Both she and her partner, Harry had an aversion towards vermin, but she didn't mention that

"Frank would be no use in the jungle, then," Dotty commented.

"So, where did he see a mouse?" Rachel asked.

"We were bonking away when he let out a loud scream and he jumped up and got dressed. He shouted out, "Did you see that, did you see that?" I didn't have a clue what he was talking about. It was most disconcerting. I'd never had remarks like that while having sex before. It was most strange because I had done nothing that might get him so excited, at least I didn't think I had." She winked.

"So, what happened next?" Rachel asked.

"He scarpered. He said he couldn't be in the same house as a mouse. I had to buy a trap.

"He wasn't called Elvis then?" Rachel looked at her friend. Kylie frowned. "Caught in a trap." Rachel's impression of Elvis was rubbish. The other two groaned.

"I'm not happy about mice in my apartment. At first, I thought he was making it up, and it was his way of saying wham bam, thank you, ma'am. Then I saw one of the little blighters jump over my waste bin." Kylie laughed.

"Oh, how awful for you. I'd have to move out if mice moved into my home."

"Yes, I suppose it's one of the drawbacks of living on the ground floor. Mind you, I believe they can crawl up pipes and everything. I will have to mention it at the next residents meeting and see if anyone else has been visited by vermin."

"I don't think Frank would take kindly to you calling him vermin." Dotty laughed.

"I will call him worse than that when I see him, that's if he comes in the pub again. He was hardly my knight in shining armour."

Kylie drained the last of her coffee and checked the time. She had shopping to do today before work tonight. Dotty was also working later in the wine bar. There was only Rachel who could relax and put her feet up with Harry and a nice glass of wine. She'd earned it after a hard week at the office. It was a good job she and Harry worked together. She told her friends how Mr Mulligan had been picking on her again and Harry had told him to lay off her. Harry worked in accounts but being an IT whizz kid, everyone respected him and wanted to use his skill and knowledge. Fred Mulligan knew not to upset Harry, so had eased off picking on Rachel.

The tea rooms were busier than usual this Saturday. There were no free tables inside and it was too cold to sit outside today. It had always been a popular little café but since the three Irish sisters took over from their mother, trade was on the up. As well as their usual customers, they had now acquired corporate clients by providing buffets. They also did speciality celebration cakes, a selection of which were on display in the window. The attention to detail of their creations with their intricate sugar and chocolate work meant they had already gained a following of happy customers. Kylie kept ribbing Rachel to get married again so she could sample one of their spectacular showcase pieces. Rachel said she had seen enough wedding cake thank you and hoped her cheating ex choked on it.

The front door opened and brought with it a gust of wind. Kylie looked across to see who was there.

"Have you seen who's walked in, Dotty? It's your neighbour, Betty with Audrey and Gladys. Betty won't be happy that there's nowhere to sit."

Kylie was right. Betty stood with her hands on her hips and her eyes narrowed.

"Here, Betty, you can have my seat. I'm ready to leave," Kylie called out. Betty toddled up to their table.

"Thank you, Kylie." Dotty downed the last of her drink feeling that she must follow suit and offer her chair to one of the other elderly women. "This is very good of you girls. You can't get a seat in this place these days for love nor money. It's not right, you know. We've been coming here for years. It's all these young yuppies taking over the place." Betty spoke loud enough for everyone to hear and didn't mind who she offended.

Betty often said unkind things. She had no filter, so was never aware of the impact her comments had. Thankfully for Dotty, her nosey neighbour had a soft spot for her, so she didn't get a tongue lashing off Betty as often as most people. Betty sidled up next to Dotty.

"You're very kind, girls." She took an embroidered handkerchief out of her brown leather handbag and blew her nose. "I hope you don't catch my germs. I've had a dreadful cold."

"I wish I'd known, Betty. I could have done some shopping for you."

"Oh, it's okay, dear. My son, Victor did an online shop for me. It's marvellous, isn't it? I mean, he lives all the way over in Oxford, yet he could still organise my shopping. A nice young man brought it round, and we chatted about his holidays."

"I'm glad you got sorted." Dotty smiled.

"How's your course going, girls?"

"Great, thanks, Betty." Dotty knew not to ask about Betty's welfare. Experience had taught her that if she mentioned anything about her health, they would never get away. Getting stuck with tales of Betty's bad back was notorious for making people miss important appointments.

"Have you heard the news about that mystery man who was killed?" Betty leaned in towards the others.

"What you mean the man trampled to death over at Devil's Bridge Farm?" Dotty was all ears.

"That's right."

"What about him?"

"Did you know that he was wearing a suit? What sort of man wears a suit to go out walking? There's something strange about the whole affair, don't you think?"

"You're right, Betty," Dotty said. "I can't imagine anyone trudging through muddy fields dressed in their Sunday best."

"No, not even you, Dotty." Kylie laughed.

"Gosh, it is a real mystery. Have they found out who he was yet?" Rachel asked.

"Not as far as I know but mark my words, I won't rest until I discover what the blazes is going on at that farm. Rumours are flying around," Betty said.

"Rumours?" Dotty questioned.

"I don't know what Ned Bristow is up to, but something is happening there. I'll keep asking questions until I find out," she said, tapping the side of her nose. The girls looked at each other and smiled. If anyone could find out any information, Betty could.

## Chapter 7

Dotty loved college. The theory could be boring but with the practical stuff, the students often had to use each other as models, so it was nice to have treatments done. Their first day in the hair salon with real customers was a memorable one. The class had been concentrating on the theory of hair. They were eager to put into practice what they had learnt. They were told that pupils from the local school were coming in and the students would wash and blow-dry their hair.

This was the first time they had been let loose on the public, so they were excited and nervous. Dotty stood outside the door of the new college salon in her black uniform waiting to be let in. This wing of the college was a recent addition to the facility. Dotty could smell the newness of the place which added to the buzz. She would be one of the first students to grace the new, state-of-the-art, award-winning salon that had been built for her education. She wondered how long its virginal state would remain. How soon would something get broken or spilt on the shiny new floor? She prayed she wouldn't be the first to spoil things. None of them knew anything about her clumsiness yet.

They had been lectured on health and safety, so Dotty knew the obvious things to watch out for. The water had to be checked on her arm for the correct temperature before spraying it on the client's head. Spillage had to be mopped up and hair swept up as soon as possible to avoid trips. She wouldn't be permitted to use scissors or bleach for some time yet, so she guessed things should be relatively hazard-free. Mrs Carling finished telling the group how to behave in front of their clients.

"Even though they are only children, I want you to treat them as you would any client. Remember, smiling faces at all times. Make sure you ask their name and build rapport by continually calling them by it. Find out about them, what their hobbies are. It is so important to build a positive relationship with your client. After you've done that, take their outer clothes to the cloakroom and gown them up. Then you must listen carefully to their instructions on how they want their hair blowing. You can suggest alternatives if you feel confident enough. Remember what you have learnt. Look at the shape of their face and go with your instincts. I will walk around to check how you are doing, so if you have any questions, just ask. Good luck everyone. Let's roll them in."

Mrs Carling rose from her chair. Dotty wondered how she stood for so long in those high-heeled shoes. Internally, her feet were probably throbbing, but she kept up her professional smile. She was only small, just over five feet tall, so the heels gave her extra height. She had an attractive face and wore her hair tied back in a bun. A thick layer of makeup highlighted her deep-lined complexion. Dotty suspected she was a smoker and was surprised she hadn't had Botox like many of the other tutors. Dotty could be critical of people's looks and that had intensified since starting her course. She felt Mrs

Carling would have benefitted from a more natural look with her makeup. The blue eye shadow she wore drew the observer in towards her laughter lines.

The tutor tottered up to the door and opened it. She waved the children in. They looked like final year junior students, aged about ten or eleven. They held consent forms from their parents in their grubby little hands. These agreed for them to have their hair done.

Dotty's model was tall for his age, so she had to adjust the chair to get the right height. That was a procedure in itself. Not being the most technical of people, it flummoxed her, so the young boy helped her find the correct lever to press.

"Thanks, I'm Dotty." She went to shake his hand. He looked nervous and didn't know what to do. Dotty quickly moved her arm away.

"Can I ask your name?" She smiled.

"Saj."

"Let me take your jacket, Saj then we'll put this gown on." Dotty was all fingers and thumbs. Even though he was only ten years old, this was still her first client. She picked up her comb and began combing his thick dark hair. It was lank and greasy. He had a long fringe and would have benefitted from a trim, but they hadn't been taught how to cut hair yet. "So how do you usually style your hair?" Dotty smiled at him through the mirror as she combed it forwards and then sideways. He appeared to have a fair bit of dandruff. Saj shrugged his shoulders and Dotty kept smiling.

They were told they needed to make product recommendations for their clients. This was an important business skill they must practise. Mrs Carling said it would show prospective employers they had all-round ability which would be an asset in boosting sales. She told them to get into this habit from the outset. For Dotty, this was the hardest part. She gulped and closed her eyes.

"I recommend our anti-dandruff shampoo for you. It will soothe your scalp. It contains natural extracts of calming lavender, mint and tea tree." Saj stared at her. Dotty felt sure he would have been more interested if she said it had extract of dinosaur dung mixed with lizard saliva.

She continued, "I'm sure you'll love it. It smells divine and it will leave your hair looking shiny and healthy afterwards." She held up the bottle to show Saj through the mirror. He was busy looking around the room. Dotty guessed what he was thinking — what have I let myself in for with this strange woman? Dotty looked across to check what everyone else was doing. She couldn't tell if any of the others had started their sales pitches on the children, but she carried on with her pre-rehearsed speech. This would surely gain her Brownie points for her enthusiasm. She gestured for Saj to move towards the sink, but he didn't respond. Still smiling, Dotty walked over to the empty chair and placed her hands on the back and shook it.

"This way please, Saj. We'll wash your hair now." With a heave, he got up and Dotty settled him into position at the wash station.

She put the towel around his shoulders and turned the taps on to test the water temperature. Her stomach churned. She wanted to get this right and make a good first attempt. She remembered to cup her hand over his forehead to avoid splashing water in his face. The tepid liquid sprayed onto his hair.

"Water ok, Saj?" He didn't reply. Dotty wondered if he might be deaf. She poured a circle of shampoo onto her palm and began to lather it into his head. Straightaway she noticed the dandruff.

Dotty massaged his scalp, building up the lather. She glanced at the snowy looking specks in his hair. Something in the back of her mind sent out a warning siren. She couldn't think what it was. She looked around the room. Everyone was busy with their clients. No one noticed her. The tutor was speaking to someone over the other side of the salon. At least that meant she wouldn't be judged on her technique on this occasion. That was a relief. Dotty looked back at Saj's hair. The dandruff looked very uniform. It wasn't isolated specks. It lay neatly in rows behind his ears. Where had she seen that before? Why was this picture ringing a bell in her mind? Suddenly, she had a moment of clarity and the memory came flooding back. She knew exactly where she had seen that sight before. In a previous lesson, they had learnt about head lice. The details came back to Dotty.

*The eggs will form in rows behind the ears. There they will lie on the shafts of hair where the temperature is perfect for keeping warm until they hatch. Lice eggs look like dandruff but brushing or shaking them off can't remove them.*

Her heartbeat quickened. Thump, thump, thump.

"Please be dandruff," she whispered under her breath. She rubbed and rubbed at the soapy lather on his head, willing the white specks to disappear. Dotty was afraid to look. She squeezed her eyes shut but when she opened them and looked down, they were still there. She felt nausea rising inside her. Adrenalin rushed through her body as the realisation sunk in. Those tiny white bits wouldn't budge.

She wanted to scream out, "nit alert, nit alert," but knew she must stay calm. She breathed deeply. Her head bobbed up and down as she tried to grab her tutor's attention. It didn't work. She had to remain in control and not alarm her client. "Don't panic, don't panic," she said under her breath. It was imperative not to embarrass him. Dotty looked around for help. Her eyes pleaded for someone to notice her awkwardness. She didn't know what to do or how to deal with this. The final part of the lesson about dealing with the head lice had been erased from her memory. She had completely forgotten what they learnt. Why didn't she listen more? She could only remember the interesting part, the photographs of the little critters. Should she stop what she was doing? She needed to catch someone's attention. Rose was the closest student and had been chatting with a young girl at the next position.

"Psst," Dotty called out. She leant over and tapped Rose's arm. Dotty mouthed to her, signalling for her to take a look without saying anything. Rose looked down then stared at Dotty with wide eyes.

"I think it's them. You'd better tell Mrs Carling," Rose whispered. From her expression, it looked like aliens had landed.

Thankfully, Mrs Carling knew what to do. They got Saj out of the salon as quickly as possible and told him the reason he was being pushed out. He got upset but Dotty tried to reassure him. She said that nits only live on clean hair and not to worry as it was very common. She prayed it wasn't too common though, and she particularly hoped they hadn't jumped in her hair. The idea of a nit infestation at this stage in her life would be most unwelcome.

The incident almost caused a crisis. They had to ship the children out as quickly as possible and fumigate the room. Dotty wouldn't forget this lesson in a hurry. At least now, she knew what head lice looked like.

Dotty met up with Kylie and James later that day. The incident was already causing a stir amongst the students. It was supposed to be confidential, but everyone had heard what happened.

"It was meant to be hush hush," Dotty said.

"Are you joking, in this place?" James mockingly scratched his own and Kylie's heads.

The three friends had become inseparable since James opened up to the girls about his past. It wasn't just the fact he showed his vulnerability. He was hilariously funny and impersonated the staff. He had their little foibles down to a tee.

"Do you make fun of people in front of Khalid?" Dotty asked James as she wiped away a tear. She had laughed so much, she cried, as he finished taking off Mrs Carling running around the salon panicking over the nits.

"Listen, just because he's royalty, it doesn't mean he's stiff upper lip. Why do you think he spends all his time out of Qatar? He spends most of his time in the UK. The reason I like him so much, as well as being well hung and having pots of money, of course, is because he's a rebel."

"Oh James, you're incorrigible." Dotty teased.

"I know, but you love me for it, don't you?"

"Yes, we do." Seeing James bringing joy to their world, it was hard to believe the mental anguish he endured in his youth. It was good to see him now enjoying his life. His stars must have gotten themselves into a more positive alignment. Hopefully, Dotty's would do the same. She scratched her head as she thought about today's harrowing experience and what may be in store for her future.

## Chapter 8

"I don't know what I'm going to do, Dotty. Paul has met someone else." Her friend snivelled down the other end of the phone.

"You were too good for him, anyway. Stick close to your friends, Dave. It will take time, but you'll get through this."

"I thought he was the one." What Dotty really wanted to say was that Paul obviously wasn't the one and that Dave should pull himself together. He had phoned her almost every day for the past week. He couldn't continue moping around. She knew it wasn't doing him any good, feeling sorry for himself. She laughed inwardly. It wasn't that many months ago when she had designs on Dave herself before he confessed that he preferred men.

"I've got an idea. Remember we said we would do some landscape painting together. How about we take a picnic and our paints and have a day out this weekend? Painting can be very therapeutic."

"I don't know if I'm in the right frame of mind to concentrate on anything."

"What's the alternative, drowning your sorrows and getting drunk? It would be a laugh. We could go down by the river while it's still warm enough. The last time I was there I fell in the water and lost my shoes in a bog. It can't be worse than that." Dotty laughed.

"Oh, you're really selling it to me now."

"Come on, Dave. I'm sure it will do you good to get out and close to nature."

"Okay, if you insist. I've got a day off next Sunday." Dave sighed. Dotty could hear the reservation in his voice but was thankful he hadn't raised any real objection. Thankfully, he couldn't see her raised eyebrows down the phone.

"Don't book in for any overtime. You need to relax more. You can't run away from your emotions by working hard forever. It will do you good to be out in the fresh air and do something creative."

She picked him up the following Sunday. He was armed with his easel, a hamper, a foldaway chair and a leather case containing his art materials. He threw everything into the boot of the car, and they drove the short journey to just past Devil's Bridge Farm and parked up.

The weather had been kind to them. The air was crisp and fresh, and the sun was out. There were clouds in the sky and grey areas in the distance which made for a dramatic setting. They carted their gear across the field and found a spot to settle.

Dave hadn't stopped talking about Paul ever since he got in the car. Apparently, Paul had now met a younger model. Dotty had heard enough of Dave's moaning. She didn't want to listen to anymore. She pitched her easel and chair up and tried to block out the sounds coming from his lips. She laid the rug on the floor and dived into the picnic hamper and took out a bottle of Prosecco.

"Here, get that down you and think about what to paint," she said, handing Dave a plastic glass full of bubbles. "I'd love to paint one of the river and get that heron in." She pointed to the bird stood patiently watching his prey.

"Why don't you take a photograph, then if he flies off you can still use it to copy from."

"Good idea." She fixed herself a glass of homemade lemonade and set out her stall. Shielding her eyes from the sun, she looked over the field where the heron stood on the embankment. Keeping her eyes on her target, she took out her phone and began snapping.

By the time she set the food out, Dave was on his third glass of wine. Dotty had been up early that morning and had made a cheese and broccoli quiche and sandwiches. Dave had offered to bring food, but she had told him to bring the drinks. He put some crisps in and sat munching the sour cream and chive Pringles.

"It's lovely here, isn't it? We're so fortunate to have all this beauty on our doorsteps." That was the first positive comment Dave had made in ages.

"Yes, I often bring Winnie out this way when it's fine. I stay closer to home when it's muddy, but I agree, there's no better place when the weather is kind to us like today. It's a shame Winnie couldn't have come but she wouldn't have behaved herself."

"It's nice to have a day off work. I've been putting in the extra hours trying to take my mind off Paul. At least my bank manager will be happy with the split."

"It's like you always say, Dave, for every negative, there's a positive to be taken out of it.

I'm sure the reason you and Paul broke up was because there is someone better out there for you. It's a matter of timing. Your time will come." As Dotty said that, she knew she needed to listen to her own words. She felt ready to settle down and meet someone, if only the right guy would come along.

They started their artwork and Dotty drew a rough sketch of what she wanted to paint. She held her hands up to get perspective for her drawing. Once she was confident that she had the right angles and everything was where it was supposed to be, she took out her paints and mixed the colours on her palette. Before long, she was engrossed in her project.

"How's your piece coming along?" she called across to Dave sat a few yards away.

"I'll show you mine if you show me yours." He laughed. Dotty thought it was good to see her friend happy again. She walked over to view his painting. He was doing a watercolour whereas she was working in acrylics.

"I love how you've got the different shades of green running into each other." She pointed to the trees he had painted. "I'm rubbish with watercolour. It always looks a splodgy mess when I try to tackle it."

"Yes, you need to be careful not to overwork your painting. Working outdoors means it dries quickly so I must look lively. Yours is coming along nicely. I love the vibrant colours in the sky that you've done." He nodded, looking closer at Dotty's work.

"Thanks, Dave. Shall we give it another hour then stop for food?"

"Sounds like a plan."

They beavered away with their painting, both getting lost in their work. Dave had to admit this had been a good call. It had taken his mind off his private life. Painting was so therapeutic. His head was filled with nothing else other than his brushstrokes and his piece of art. He picked up his initial pencil sketch and compared it to his painting. He needed to get more depth in. Screwing up his eyes, he rose from his seat and looked at his work from a distance. The wind was getting up and kept flicking over his pad.

Dotty checked her watch. She couldn't believe the time. It was almost three. They were so wrapped up in their work, they had forgotten to eat.

"It's about time we tucked into this lot," Dotty said rummaging through the hamper basket and taking out the paper plates. She set out the Tupperware boxes filled with rice and pasta salads.

"Gosh, you've done us proud. This spread is fit for a king."

"Only the best for you, Dave." Dotty laughed.

"Mm, this quiche is good. You must give me the recipe." Not only did the two friends have a common interest in art, but they also both loved good food.

"Sure thing."

Dave wolfed the food down then finished off the last of the wine and lay sprawled out on the tartan rug. Within minutes, he was snoring gently. Dotty smiled. It would do him no harm to catch up on his sleep. She packed away the empty tubs and settled back in her chair ready to complete her painting. The heron had long since moved on, but she spotted a gaggle of geese in the neighbouring field so took out her phone and snapped them. Having eaten more than she intended, her eyes drooped. The afternoon sun beat down on her face and before long she too settled down to rest her eyes. She dozed off.

Dotty came to just in time to catch the sun setting. Again, she took out her camera. Beyond the meadow was Ned Bristow's farm, and she spotted two cars driving up his lane. Thinking no more of it, she got herself comfortable, ready to complete her work. Dave stirred and when he opened his eyes, he couldn't remember where he was at first. He looked disorientated.

"How long have I been asleep?" he asked as he rose from the rug and brushed the grass from his jeans.

"I'm not sure. I nodded off as well."

"It's going dark. I think it's time we called it a day. I'll finish my piece off at home."

"Yeah, I've just about completed mine," Dotty said, stretching out her arms. "Come on, let's put everything away." Most of their equipment was packed, so there wasn't much to do. The friends made their way back to Dotty's car.

Being a policeman taught Dave to be on the alert. He noticed several cars going into Ned Bristow's farm. Dotty followed his gaze.

"Ned must be having another party or something," she commented. Dave nodded but kept his eyes trained on the convoy of vehicles. "Has there been any more news on the poor man who died there?" Dotty asked.

"I believe he's from the Middle East."

"Oh?"

"I don't know any more than that. They've not put a name to him yet."

"I see."

## Chapter 9

"Have you done any revising for your first assessment?" James asked Kylie. James joined the girls at their favourite café for their weekly get together.

"Are you joking? It's only a practical. What do we need to study?" Kylie looked aghast.

"Apparently, they ask questions while they watch you work."

"Oh no, I didn't know that. I mustn't have been listening when we were told." Kylie put her hand over her mouth. "Did you know, Dotty?"

"Yes, the tutor mentioned it. I wouldn't worry, the questions will be easy."

"They may be easy for you but I'm not so sure. Go on test me."

Rachel arrived at the same time as Stella the waitress placed a cafetiere of coffee on the table.

"Can we have an extra mug, please? There should be enough for you, Rachel." She sat down.

"What must you always do before colouring a client's hair?" James asked.

"Oh, that's easy, a skin test to check for allergic reactions."

"When cutting a client's hair, and you're working on the left side, do you put the weight on your left foot, lean over or balance on both feet equally?" Dotty quizzed.

"Balance on both feet, of course. That question sounds silly."

"How does a hairdresser win a race?" Rachel asked, smiling.

"I don't know."

"By taking a short cut." Rachel laughed at her own joke.

"Milly told me the question about standing on both legs was asked in the exam. If you have common sense you can answer most of them," Dotty said.

"That's got you scuppered then, Dotty." Kylie laughed.

"Oy, cheeky."

"Have you seen anything of Milly lately?" Rachel asked. Milly had previously done the hair and beauty course and encouraged Dotty to go back to college. She told her how much she loved working in the industry. It had been enough to convince Dotty that this was the right career choice for her after years of indecision and indifference to work.

"No, we keep planning to meet and then something comes up."

"You've not taken your dogs out together again, have you?"

"No, that was disastrous." Dotty explained to James that her little poodle, Winnie went for Milly's big Great Dane, Schmeichel when they were out walking once. The result was that Milly got pulled through the mud by Schmeichel and ruined her cream coat.

"More fool her for wearing cream."

"Poor Schmeichel hasn't been so well lately. Milly found a lump on his back."

"Oh dear, that doesn't sound good." James took out a lip balm and checking in a tiny silver-plated mirror, dabbed some on his lips. "Does anyone want to try this? It has special lip plumping qualities."

Kylie scooped a small amount onto her finger.

"Oo, it tastes nice."

"I bet she says that to all the boys." James winked.

"Don't be saucy, James. I only have eyes for you." The two friends blew each other a kiss.

James sat back and breathed in the heavenly smell of freshly brewed coffee. He looked around the café. A queue of people waited for tables. A group of older women stood at the counter ogling the cakes.

"This place is a little gold mine, isn't it?"

"Oh yes, they do well but the family work hard, so they deserve it. Talking of gold mines, when are we going to meet that prince of yours?" Kylie winked at her friend. He didn't seem offended by her comments.

"Khalid is out of the country a lot. He doesn't just have the apartment in Sussex, you know. He has a place in Paris and the palace in his home, Qatar. Being a prince brings a great deal of responsibility. He has to count his oil rigs or whatever it is he does to them."

"I reckon he sits there counting out his lovely lolly. That's what I would do all day if I was rich. I'd sit there checking every last penny." Kylie licked her finger and pretended to count notes. "Does he spend much of his money on you?"

"Kylie, don't be so personal." Dotty opened her eyes wide and glared at her friend.

"I wondered if James got lots of nice expensive presents from his lover. I mean, it's not worth having a rich partner if he doesn't shower you in gifts, is it?" Dotty shook her head.

"It's okay, I know what she's like. I've been around her long enough now." James smiled. "He bought me this watch, but I prefer him to show me how much he loves me rather than buy me gifts." It was hard to miss James' Rolex as the gold gleamed on his wrist. "Anyway, in answer to your question, Kylie, we're arranging a soiree for Khalid's birthday. You'll be invited, of course, so you can meet him then."

"What's a soiree when it's at home?" Kylie asked.

"Oh, Kylie, don't be so uncouth. It's a posh name for a party, isn't it, James?" James laughed.

Dotty and Kylie discussed their impending exams, and they both groaned at the prospect. Neither of them could naturally apply themselves to swatting the way James did. The girls found it difficult to remember things. Dotty had been particularly bad at dates in history even though she loved the subject matter. She couldn't even recall what she ate for her evening meal the previous night, never mind what happened in 1066. James said he would help them by continuing to test them at college. He was a dream student but far too keen for their liking. Kylie, especially, wanted to pass using the minimum effort.

Dotty took a slurp of coffee as her phone rang. She looked at the caller's name. It was Milly. That was a coincidence after just talking about her. She wondered if Milly was ringing about Schmeichel. She anticipated the worst. Dotty answered on the second ring.

"Hi, Milly." All Dotty could hear the other end was sobbing. "Milly?" Eventually, the sniffles stopped, and Milly spoke.

"I'm sorry, Dotty. I have been so worried about Schmeichel. He's been coughing up blood and not eating, so I took him to the vets. I've got the results of a blood test back. It's cancer, Dotty."

"Is there anything that can be done?"

"He can have surgery and the vet may suggest chemo depending if they can remove everything. I'm concerned, Dotty. He's only ten and I've had him since he was a puppy. I don't want to lose him." Dotty thought how she would feel if anything happened to Winnie. It would be like losing a sibling.

"I don't know what to say, Milly. I'm so sorry. If there's anything I can do, don't hesitate to ask."

"I don't want him to be in pain. He's not been wagging his tail. It's not like him."

"Just do what's best for Schmeichel. I don't think chemo is as bad as it is for humans. Dogs don't usually lose their fur. You've got pet insurance, haven't you?"

"No, I've not. I forgot to renew it. My parents have offered to foot the bill. They know how much Schmeichel means to me."

By the time they ended the call, Dotty felt low herself. She went online to google cancer in dogs for her friend. She wanted to know the symptoms in case anything happened to Winnie as she was a similar age to Schmeichel.

"Cheer up, Dotty. You've got exams to look forward to." Rachel's idea of a joke fell flat. How could she identify with what Milly was going through? Rachel only had a pet parrot to worry about.

## Chapter 10

Schmeichel only lived for another two weeks. The cancer was further advanced than they anticipated. It gave Milly little time to adjust. It wasn't easy for her to come to terms with the death of her beloved dog. The only blessing was he didn't suffer for long. He became listless, and she sat there for hours stroking him. In the end, it was as though he knew his time had come. He wanted to isolate and not go out. When he died, Milly found him curled up under a bush in the garden. It wasn't the one he usually napped under. Milly thought it was because he didn't want to go to his special place and ruin the happy memories of the tree that he loved to play near. She guessed he didn't have long when he wouldn't play with his favourite squeezy doll. He had already lost interest in food and it was a struggle for her to get him to drink. Even when he ate, he often vomited it back. His breathing became ragged. There was lots of panting, then great pauses followed by a rattling sound. Milly found it difficult to watch, but she stayed in touch with Dotty. Before Schmeichel went off to the bush to die, he went up to Milly for a last pet. It was as though he had sixth sense, and it was how he wanted to say goodbye.

Milly had planned Schmeichel's funeral. It was held in her back garden and she invited friends and family. She had set out an area where she displayed photos of Schmeichel together with his lead and collar and his favourite toy. She even wrote a short poem as a way of remembering him. It was very poignant.

Dotty was there with Kylie and another friend of Kylie's from college, Candice. Candice looked like Kylie's double. They were in the same group and along with James, Candice had become good friends with Kylie. Candice wore her hair short and cropped, similar to Kylie's. Candice's locks had been long and dark when she started the course. They were told that in order to progress with hairdressing they would need to allow experimentation on themselves. That meant having their hair cut and coloured by the other students.

"Over my dead body," Dotty said. She still hadn't given in to changing her appearance. Her long auburn hair was still coiffured in the same style made synonymous with the forties and fifties era. Dotty had no desire to change the look as she loved it. Kylie often liked to change her hair colour or at least the streak at the front. It had been pink, blue and purple and she was happy to continue doing so. Candice's change in appearance was drastic. She was a large girl, a similar frame to Kylie. Now they both had short cropped platinum blonde hair and today they both wore a blue streak at the front. They could easily pass for sisters, or twins even. Candice started wearing false lashes and fake tan like Kylie.

At first, Kylie was flattered by the changes Candice made. She felt she must be doing something right if the girl wanted to copy her. But Candice's hero-worship of Kylie was becoming obsessive. Whatever colour Kylie changed her hair to, Candice did the same. Initially, when Candice asked her about changing the shade, Kylie told her what she had planned but lately, she had become sneaky on purpose to avoid having a double. If Kylie had known what the rest of the class had nicknamed the pair of friends, she would have been mortified. Behind their backs, the others sniggered and called them Tweedledum and Tweedledee.

Another similarity was the way the two girls drank. Candice knocked them back in similar proportions to Kylie. Both Rachel and Dotty were lightweights in comparison, so Kylie was glad to have a companion who didn't make her heavy drinking sessions look as bad. Candice started coming in the Six Bells on a Friday night and she and Kylie went out afterwards. It was often the case on Monday morning at college that neither girl could remember exactly where they had been. They just knew it had been a good night as their hangovers told them so. Candice hadn't met Milly before. When Kylie told her about the poor animal's demise, she invited herself to the dog's funeral. She owned a little spaniel and felt sorry for Milly, plus she knew there would be drink involved.

Milly played some music on her phone that she said was Schmeichel's favourite. It was, "Who let the dogs out." With its upbeat tempo, the small crowd jigged along and tapped their feet. The dark clouds overhead threatened to spoil the short event, so Milly made the service even shorter before the rain pelted down.

"Come on, let's head indoors and crack open a bottle of wine," she called out.

"That was a lovely service," Dotty said as she shook the water off her jacket.

"I'm sure Schmeichel would have been proud of what you did for him," Kylie added. Milly blinked a tear away and Kylie handed her a tissue. "Will you get another dog?"

"I don't know yet. It's too early to say. If I do, it won't be a big dog like Schmeichel. Before he got ill, he had a healthy appetite, and it cost me a small fortune. I'd go for something smaller if I get another dog."

"I think you should get one. You love animals and it would help you deal with your loss." Milly's mum smiled as she joined the circle of friends stood in the kitchen. "I believe Ned Bristow breeds collie puppies. Why don't you have a word with him?"

"I love collies and they're such an obedient dog normally." She nodded. "You've got me thinking."

"I could always treat you for your birthday if that's what you decide, darling. A dog would be expensive, but it would be my treat." Milly's mum held onto her daughter's arm.

"Thanks, Mum. It's sweet of you. I will seriously think about it in the future. For now, I need time to grieve over Schmeichel."

## Chapter 11

"Come on, Kylie keep it up. Exercise releases serotonin. Dr Chris said on the telly that it is as vital for the brain as it is for the body." Dotty puffed out as she spoke.

"Slow down, can't you?" Kylie stopped running and bent over with her hands on her knees. "This is killing me. I haven't done cross-country since I was at school. It's okay for you. You walk regularly with Winnie but I'm too unfit to do anything like jogging. I'm sure we'd be better sat indoors revising rather than prancing around out here making fools of ourselves."

Dotty jogged on the spot. Her subtle dark blue velour tracksuit was a stark contrast to Kylie's loud cerise pink affair. If Kylie didn't want to be seen, she had hardly worn the correct attire. She didn't exactly blend in with the passing scenery. It was early evening, and the sky had turned an inky blue.

"This is excellent for your health and you may lose a few pounds into the bargain."

"I have started a diet."

"Good for you. What diet are you doing?"

"Oh, so far, I've only given up salt."

"Oh, Kylie, what are you like. Mind you it's a start. Too much salt is bad for your heart. It can cause high blood pressure and strokes."

"Do you have to be so cheerful?"

"Are you ready to set off again?" Dotty was eager to continue.

"Can't we walk? Walking will do me as much good."

"Why don't we try to walk a tree, run a tree?"

"What?"

"Come on, do what I do." Dotty beckoned her friend forward. "You only need run as far as the first tree then walk to the next one."

"But the next tree is miles away."

"No, it's not. You'll feel great when you've finished. Look, your cheeks have got a nice rosy glow."

"That's from too much alcohol."

"Well if it is then this will work the poison out of your pores and if you like I can ask you questions and test you while we run."

There was only so far Dotty could push her friend before she gave up completely.

"I can't run and concentrate." The girls finally slowed to a walking pace.

"Don't you feel better already?"

"Not at the moment, no. I feel I'm about to have a coronary. I suppose I will reap the benefit in about a week when I'm over the pain of using muscles I didn't know existed. I can't see me keeping this up regularly. How do people enjoy this?" A rising feeling of nausea crept up inside Kylie's chest. She stood and leaned against a tree. "I think I've done too much."

"You'll be fine. Have a drink of water." Kylie took her water bottle out of her small matching pink rucksack. "Keep this up and you'll soon see muscles instead of fat." Dotty wiped the perspiration from her brow. She continued jogging on the spot. "I've enjoyed it even if you haven't and it's good to run together. It helps to motivate us."

"Yes, you're right. If I want to grab myself a decent fella, he won't want all this blubber." Kylie grabbed hold of the spare tyre around her midriff.

"Well, if that's the motivation you need, stick with it. Whatever it takes to get you exercising more."

"I can't believe I let you talk me into this. Being this sweaty is gross."

"Think of all those calories oozing out of your pores."

Kylie pulled a face. Dotty laughed and shook her head. They walked along the path at the side of the meadow. The long grass bent over in the breeze. Dark shadows loomed in front, created by the hedges and trees. The only sound was of the leaves rustling as the branches swayed. Dotty glanced over in the distance. The sound of car engines disturbed their peace. She frowned as she watched several cars travel up the lane to Devil's Bridge Farm.

"Looks like Ned Bristow is having another party."

"How come we never get an invitation?" Kylie watched the cars drive along the road.

"I don't know him that well, thank goodness. The way that he treated James, I don't want to know him."

"Yeah, but if there's free booze, I don't mind who is providing it."

"What happened to your healthy new lifestyle?" The girls peered over the hedgerow to get a closer look. They could see people walking out towards the far field.

"It looks like he must be having a barbecue. They're all congregating outside." Dotty's eyes narrowed.

"It's a bit cold for a barbecue, but I could murder a drink."

"What, and undo all this good work?"

"The odd glass of wine won't do me any harm."

"When have you ever stuck to the odd glass?"

"Well, the odd bottle then. There are some tasty looking cars going up Ned's driveway. I've spotted a Merc, a Porsche and an Audi. He must have some mates with money."

"I wonder if they are fellow farmers. If so, it looks like it's not a bad little earner."

The friends made their way back along the track towards the houses. At the end of the field, they parted company after a brief hug.

"See you at college."

"Let me know if you want to come for another run, Kylie."

"I'll be aching for a week after this little spurt of energy. I can think of better ways to burn off calories." She winked.

"What are you like? See you later." Dotty shook her head and set off jogging back towards her house. As she drew up close, she spotted her neighbour, Betty, about to get into a car. Betty waved her over, so Dotty ran across.

"Good for you going for a run. I'm off to a music recital with Gladys. I hope the seats aren't too hard. I don't want them putting my back out again."

"Have a good time, Betty."

"Thanks. Have you heard the news?"

"What news is that?"

"About the man killed by cattle up at the farm."

"No, what's that then?"

"They've found out where he was from." It never ceased to amaze Dotty how Betty found out so much but there again, she knew everyone and loved a good gossip.

"Oh, and where's that then?"

"Qatar in the Middle East."

"Really?" Dotty raised her eyebrows.

"You look surprised. Does that mean anything to you?" The cogs in Dotty's brain whirred around. When Dave mentioned the dead man was from the Middle East, she hadn't registered but suddenly a thought came to her.

"No, it's unusual, that's all. Have a nice night, Betty." Dotty turned and ran up towards her home. She didn't want to say too much to Betty as it may only be a coincidence. Betty was likely to put two and two together and make five. What was interesting to Dotty was that James' lover was also from Qatar. Did they know each other?

## Chapter 12

It didn't take much persuasion to convince Milly to get another dog. The hole left by Schmeichel created a void in her heart. Her Great Dane played such a large part in Milly's wellbeing that it was crazy not to realise that a pup could fill that gap. She researched where and what to buy. Finally, she chose Ned Bristow. He was a local breeder who she knew of, so didn't question his credentials. She fancied getting a collie. Another big dog was out of the question and she didn't like small dogs so a medium size pet would suit her fine. Intelligent and athletic, collies made good family dogs. Having made her mind up, she phoned Ned. He told her he had the perfect puppy for her. She couldn't wait to meet the new addition to her family. It was as exciting for her as Christmas day. In Milly's opinion, dogs were more loyal than men and she looked forward to having a new companion.

She took her mum along for the ride and they drove out towards the farmhouse. Devil's Bridge Farm was an old stone building with brickwork of sombre grey. Tall, neatly trimmed pine trees shaded the farm from the main road. The front garden had an abundance of trimmed rose bushes. The pristine front lawn with the uniform flower beds told of a keen gardener who'd been at work there. Milly glanced out into the field where the cattle lay grazing and shuddered as she thought about the recent tragic accident that occurred there.

She parked up and the two women climbed out of Milly's vehicle. Glad she wore her wellies, they trampled through muddy patches past a brand-new Range Rover and up to the front steps of the main building. The heavy oak front door looked ostentatious with its brass nameplate.

When the doorbell rang, the theme tune to *EastEnders* sounded and Milly raised her eyebrows. She detested tackiness. A cold wind blew across the moorland. Her mum stamped her feet and zipped up her coat as they waited for someone to open the door. Milly thrust her hands deep into her pockets. No one answered. Milly frowned and knocked on the large brass door knocker with its lion's head staring back at them and waited. Taking in the area, Milly noticed that the main farmhouse had numerous extensions attached. They were a mismatch of various brickwork buildings that had obviously been added at different stages in the smallholding's history. There were blocks of outhouses including barns either side. The original building now looked awkward but large. Some may have been impressed by its size, but not Milly. A cockerel crowed and set off a cacophony of dogs barking. Milly smiled and wondered which bark would be the one of her soon-to-be new pet.

"Sounds like he has a lot of dogs to choose from." Milly rubbed her hands together. A small young woman in her twenties finally answered the door. Her face looked blank but there were signs of strain around her mouth and eyes.

"Hi, we've come about the puppy. Ned's expecting us." Milly raised her eyebrows. The woman's expression didn't change. Her honey-coloured complexion and matching hair didn't follow through to her welcome.

"Wait there." She closed the door in Milly's face. Milly turned to her mum and shrugged her shoulders.

"She won't win any awards for her hospitality, whoever she is."

"She obviously went to the same charm school as Ned himself." The door creaked open again and Ned stood there. Milly's heart skipped a beat and she hoped he hadn't overheard her mum's comment.

The first thing she noticed was Ned's bulky frame. As her eyes wandered up to his face, she focused on his rugged weather-beaten cheeks highlighting his broken nose. He looked like a classic farmer. He may have been large, but he certainly wasn't jolly. His face was a picture of annoyance. He frowned when Milly introduced her and her mum. He wasn't impressed by the two women who disturbed his peace or whatever it was he was doing. Milly told him what time they'd be there, but that didn't seem to matter to Ned. She explained to him how her beloved dog, Schmeichel recently died. If she had been hoping for empathy or to connect with him through a love of animals, it hadn't worked. He cut her off.

"I told you over the phone how much it would cost, didn't I?"

"Yes, and we've brought cash as you asked."

Ned sneered and grunted, mumbling to himself. Milly felt so uncomfortable. The sooner she chose a puppy and got out of there the better.

He wanted to see the colour of her money before he showed her the dogs which seemed odd.

"You can't be too careful. I've had time wasters before, people trying to con me in the past." His jaw clenched. The frown he wore looked like a permanent fixture. Milly wished now that Dotty hadn't told her how Ned treated his son. It affected her feelings towards him which couldn't be less favourable.

"Quite." Milly shifted her weight onto her other foot as she stood waiting to be shown some puppies.

"Are you sure it's a collie you want? I've got a lovely spaniel as well."

"No, I've decided I would like a collie dog."

"Stay there. Vanessa will bring the dog in." Ned was abrupt with his tone. Milly was surprised. She expected to have more than one dog to choose from. They waited in the high-ceilinged hall. The floor was tiled in black and white Italian porcelain. Ned disappeared and eventually, Vanessa brought through a tiny mite of a thing. Milly's heart melted. Those almond eyes looked longingly at her.

"I hear they are a sweet-natured, gentle breed." Dotty smiled at Vanessa as Ned walked back in the room. The young girl's expression was blank. She didn't reply. Ned signalled for them to follow him into a drawing-room. Vanessa followed them in with the dog. The decor was traditional with deep pile dark red patterned carpet. The antiques could have been expensive for all Milly knew. In her opinion, they were spoilt by an array of dismal looking oil paintings.

They were shown to a leather seat that was weathered and scratched and Milly and her mum both perched on the end. Milly couldn't stop glancing at the main painting over the fireplace. A young nude woman graced the picture. She found looking at all that flesh disconcerting and not to her taste. She turned back towards the small animal, and cocked her head, itching to stroke the little dog.

"How old did you say she was?"

"Eleven weeks." Ned's tone was curt. "Her name is Tara."

"Is it possible to see her mother?" Milly's mum asked.

"This one's from the first litter. The mother didn't take to her, so we broke them up."

"Oh, oh, I see. Can I hold her?" Vanessa passed the puppy to Milly who noticed that the dog's nose was crusty."

"Is everything okay with her health?"

"Yes, she's had a bit of a cold, that's all." Ned was busy counting his cash. At that point, Milly should have listened to her instincts. Something inside told her not to progress with the sale but she had already fallen for the little puppy. Reluctantly, Milly took the receipt from Ned, and they left. If she hadn't been so eager to get a new dog and so keen to be out of Ned's way, then she may have taken greater heed of the warning signs. However, the dog looked so cute and it was hard for Milly to resist those doleful eyes.

"Come on, Tara, let's get you home."

It was Milly's mum who made an interesting observation on the way out.

"Ned Bristow only seemed bothered about getting your money. If you ask me, he wasn't interested in the welfare of Tara at all."

"At least she's coming to a good home now. She'll be well looked after."

Milly was excited about her purchase and phoned Dotty to tell her about her experience.

"The more I hear about that man, the less I like him. It's poor James I feel sorry for. Fancy having a dad who is so rude and obnoxious. Sadly, James is lumbered with his dad but the fact they are estranged seems a blessing." Dotty thought about her own dad and for all his faults, she wouldn't change him for the world.

# Chapter 13

On Thursday evening, Dotty had a night off from the wine bar and she agreed to go for a drink with Dave. He was chattier than of late and seemed back to his old self.

"How is your bar work going?" he asked as he sipped the top of the froth off his pint of lager.

"I'm enjoying it. I've not actually seen anyone famous yet. The celebs must come in when it's my night off." She laughed. "Financially, though, I'm only just getting by. I've been looking around for another little part-time job."

"You'll have your work cut out, with studying as well."

"We don't have to be at college all the time. Even when we are there, generally, it is more like a holiday being pampered and practised on. Also, because I love the course so much, it doesn't feel like a chore. I think physically I could cope with some more hours somewhere."

"Do you plan to get another bar job?"

"Actually, I saw an advert on the noticeboard at college asking for cleaners to clean the building. It's an hour before college starts and two hours after. That shouldn't be too hard."

"Go for it, if it will help with your money situation." Dave took another swig of his drink. "Did I tell you I've been assigned to helping the coroner's office finding out who the dead man found at Devil's Bridge Farm was?"

"No, that sounds interesting."

"Yes, quite. Now it has been established that he wasn't British, I've been liaising with the Consular Office."

"Has no one reported him missing, as far as you know?"

"Because he was from a foreign country, it's not as straightforward and everything takes so much longer processing the inquiries. The language barrier doesn't help."

"You mean you don't speak any Arabic?" Dotty laughed. "Your work is very diverse, isn't it, Dave?"

"Yes, and I prefer the practical side of things. I hate it when I get bogged down with paperwork. Take this death for instance, there are so many forms to complete just to speak to someone. Then Arabic looks more like double Dutch to me. Thankfully, I've found myself a good contact and I've got a meeting at the consular affairs department at the Qatar embassy in London next week."

"That sounds very highbrow. It isn't run-of-the-mill stuff finding a body when no one's reported the person missing."

"Someone may have but it's a case of joining up the dots. Sometimes, the process seems so slow but at least we're getting somewhere. I've heard of incidents where bodies have never been identified. That must be frustrating once you reach a dead end."

"Oh well, good luck with your investigations. I hope you discover who he was, if only for his family's sake. I still think it's strange. Are the police treating it as suspicious?"

"It wasn't a natural death, so our job is to investigate as fully as we can. The coroner will decide if he thinks there has been any wrongdoing."

"I'm sure you can't get cows to stampede to order or anything like that, but I know if it was me, I'd have my concerns. I mean, what was a man in a suit doing walking on Ned Bristow's land?"

"About the stampede, the Health and Safety Executive will look into the fatal accident. They will examine everything fully which takes time and we are doing our own investigations. Old Ned won't be happy, as I expect they will be thorough and check through his accounts and procedures now regarding the cattle."

"From what I've heard about Ned Bristow, I don't like the man. Something wasn't right with what happened. I hope you find out who the poor victim was. I don't believe there were any witnesses to his death."

"Has Betty Simpson been filling you in again? That woman needs to keep her nose out of police business. She's forever meddling."

"Maybe so, but if it makes it a safer environment for the locals, then I for one will be supporting her. I believe she is involved with setting up a meeting to discuss what can be done to stop anything like the tragic accident happening again."

"I suppose you're right. The least Ned should be doing is putting up signs to warn people about the dangers of cattle. Recommendations will come out of the reports."

"Yeah, the locals will know now of the dangers but anyone from out of the area needs to be aware of the risks of walking near the farm. I don't know what Ned Bristow might be up to, but I have a hunch, there is more going on at that farm than meets the eye. Rumours are flying around."

"Oh, such as?"

"I haven't heard anything concrete. As you are aware, Betty's my main source of information. Twice, when I've walked past the farm, there has been a lot of activity there. It looks like Ned throws regular wild parties or something."

"There's nothing illegal in that."

"Can't the police put more man-hours on him to find out what he is up to?"

"Unfortunately, police budgets don't stretch to such luxuries. In an ideal world, we could check up on him but as far as we know, he hasn't done anything wrong."

"I think he should be watched." Dotty's mouth went down at the corners. Dave's views and that of the police were to let sleeping dogs lie. Dotty was like a dog with a bone and wanted to find out what was going on.

"I hope you're not planning on getting yourself involved with things that have nothing to do with you."

"No, of course not." Dotty wouldn't look Dave in the eye. He didn't know that her fingers were crossed behind her back. If the police wouldn't investigate Ned Bristow, then she would. She had taken an instant dislike to the man and secretly hoped he was doing something illegal and would get his comeuppance. It was the principal of the matter. If he was up to no good, then he shouldn't get away with it. His behaviour made a laughing stock of the local community. Dave watched Dotty's expression. He knew her too well by now to figure she wouldn't be letting this matter lie.

"I mean it, Dotty. If you get involved, it could be dangerous. You don't know what you are getting into."

"Oh, so you agree you think something dodgy is going on at Ned's farm?"

"I didn't say that." Dave looked cross now. He frowned. "Keep out of it, Dotty and leave any investigating up to the police.

How often had she been told that? Dotty wasn't good at doing as she was told.

## Chapter 14

Saturday night at the Six Bells was in full swing. A few regulars were in, along with several couples who didn't mind missing prime time TV and still liked to go out at the weekend. There was also a crowd of blokes who'd travelled over from East Grinstead for a mate's fortieth birthday bash. The birthday guy was unsteady on his feet. He was well and truly sozzled already and it wasn't even nine o'clock.

Business was booming in the pub and no one quite understood why. Other local hostelries in the area were going under, yet the Six Bells was thriving. The food was mediocre, but it was good enough for Kylie. If she didn't have time to eat before she left for work, she would nip in the pub's kitchen and pinch a few chips. Graham, the landlord wasn't impressed. He was an energetic man who wore glasses and still liked to go for early morning runs, even though he was now in his mid-fifties. From the garish Hawaiian-themed shirts he wore you might be mistaken for thinking he was gay but that was far from the truth. He loved the company of ladies and had often played away. He had a roving eye and couldn't help himself. His wife Gail continued to look the other way with his philandering because she enjoyed the prosperity his business interests brought. Tonight, though, they weren't on speaking terms. Kylie didn't wish to ask why. She could guess. Graham had been like a dog on heat since the new barmaid, Raquel started. She was in her late forties but dressed much younger. Tonight, she wore a low-cut black t-shirt that showed off her ample bosom and her many tattoos. Her fair hair was cut in a sharp bob and with her bright red lipstick, Kylie thought she looked like a sexy Russian chasing after a British husband. Graham couldn't keep his eyes off her breasts and Gail couldn't take her eyes off Graham leering at Raquel's physique.

Raquel grinned. She knew full well the effect she had on men. She was a temptress, a tease who loved to string men along. Her motto was to never get too close to get hurt yet close enough to have gifts bestowed on her. She was good at making plenty of tips and as the pot was shared out at the end of the evening, Kylie looked forward to working with her.

Raquel had finished serving the birthday crowd. It was a large order. They'd all wanted shots as well as their beers. It was then that Kylie noticed the handsome stranger. She felt his eyes on her in her peripheral vision but when she turned to look, he quickly glanced away. He had dark greasy hair and three-day stubble. His jeans were scruffy and for that reason, she didn't think he was with the celebratory group because he made no effort. But she was wrong. When she spotted him talking to one of the party of men, she was intrigued. She watched as he crossed the crowded room carrying a couple of pints. He was good-looking, yet there was something dark and mysterious about him. His hair was long, falling on his shoulders, and he wore glasses on his head. The way he carried himself, he could have been a rock star, full of ego and bravado.

Whatever was going on for Kylie, she knew she couldn't ignore it. The butterflies were doing somersaults inside. She had to get to know him, so she used her powers of charm and manipulation. She offered to go out and collect glasses. He stood chatting to an older man over the other side of the room as she brushed past him.

"The name's Will," he whispered in her ear. She rarely got nervous around men but this one had done something to her. She felt giddy with excitement, touched with a smidgeon of fear.

"I'm Kylie. I'd shake your hand but I'm carrying empties."

"Maybe when you're not carrying empties, you can shake more than my hand." Kylie felt Will's hot breath on her neck.

Kylie gulped. What she would usually say would be, "watch it, cheeky." Instead, she didn't speak. She rolled her tongue slowly around her lips. Will's eyes lit up. "Anytime." She slinked back to her position behind the bar, but as she approached the wooden frame, she turned to see if he was watching her. He was, so she winked at him. Her heart thumped like it was about to explode out of her chest. They stared at each other. She reached the other side of the bar and found it difficult to concentrate on anything. Kylie always liked to think of herself as the devourer when it came to men. It was her motto to treat 'em mean to keep 'em keen but most of the time she only gave back as good as she got. In her fantasies, she was a femme fatale and seductress but deep down she was just a girl looking for love. Because she didn't expect to find it anytime soon, she settled for fun instead. What she failed to realise was the type of guys she attracted, those out after a good time, were not the kind she could take home to meet her mum. They were not the settling down sort.

Kylie had always been the flirty type. Chasing the opposite sex had constantly been a game to her — up until now. Somehow, she knew instantly that meeting Will had changed everything. She was putty in his hands. Whatever he wanted her to do, she would oblige. She couldn't help herself. It was that simple. She was lost in a sea far deeper than pure lust. Will had got in and messed with her heart and soul.

She couldn't wait to get to know him. Even if he was married, that wouldn't matter. She had to have this man. Kylie had always been good at taking charge of situations. Tonight, was no exception. The other bar staff were happy to let her collect the glasses as Toby, the usual lad who did it, hadn't turned up. Kylie vowed to buy Toby a pint next time she saw him for giving her this opportunity. She made her way out towards where Will was talking to two men.

He pulled her into his chest. When he touched her hand, the hairs on the back of her neck stood to attention. His stubble tickled her ear sending ripples of delight cascading through her body. Something about him intimidated her, and she guessed that he knew that. She thought he must be able to read her mind and know that she had already fallen under his spell. One touch from Will and he would electrocute her or something worse. He smelled of danger and she loved it.

Kylie wasn't impressed with money. For her, it was a bonus if they could afford to wine and dine her. What was more important was that men could satisfy her in bed. They had to be good lovers, or she got rid of them. It used to be a deciding factor whether she wanted to hang out with someone that they had to have a job. As the economic climate worsened, it wasn't practical to expect all her suitors to be in gainful employment, so, she changed the criteria. From then it was if they weren't working then they must be looking for work. As the state of the nation worsened even further, she had to rethink that stipulation. Her rule became if their parents worked, she would still go out with them as they must be from good stock, with a good work ethic. In truth, Kylie didn't give two hoots about their social standing. She once went out with someone who told her he had been an armed robber and held up several off-licence shops. When Rachel quizzed her as to why she would put up with that, she answered that he made her laugh. She drew the line when he went back to prison and she didn't offer to wait for him coming out. So, when Will told her he had a job, she was pleasantly surprised.

"What is it you do?"

"I work as a farm labourer." Kylie liked the sound of that. If he did a physical job, he was likely to be well ripped. Hopefully, she may get to feel his muscles sometime soon.

"Oh, anywhere close by?"

"Yes, I work at Devil's Bridge Farm."

"Ah, that's where the man was trampled to death by cattle." Kylie watched to see how he responded.

"That's right." Will raised his eyebrows and smirked. Kylie wondered if there was anything behind his expression, but she dismissed pursuing it as she was keen to know what his intentions with her were. The way he was so tactile and couldn't keep his hands off her, she guessed she was in luck. As his hands circled her waist, she realised he was interested. As much as she wanted to play it cool, she couldn't wait to get him back to her place.

"I'll see you later when I finish working." She blew him a kiss.

"I can't wait." He tapped her butt as she walked past.

## Chapter 15

Dotty applied for and got the job cleaning the college. The work was easy once she was shown how to use the industrial equipment. The hardest part was getting up for the morning shifts. If she had worked the previous evening in the wine bar, she struggled to motivate herself. It soon became apparent that she had taken on too many hours, but she couldn't deny that the money came in handy. She could be more frivolous with her money, buying things she loved such as makeup and new clothes. She could also save for her holidays. When she added up the hours she was doing, she realised that she was working full time as well as attending college. Something had to give but for now, she managed her tiredness as best she could.

It was a good thing there were no bosses about when she did her evening shift at the college as she whizzed around with the big commercial sweeper. By that time of night, she was flagging. She zoomed down the corridors like greased lightning, so she could relax and get her head down for twenty minutes in one of the classrooms. This bad habit went on for a few weeks until Mo joined the workforce. When the older woman started as a cleaner, Dotty's cushy number lost its appeal. Previously, she got away with having a little cat nap, but these days Mo came snooping like a tiger on the prowl. She was only a cleaner, not a supervisor, but she liked to think she was in charge and she tried to boss Dotty around. She had visions of running the place and from the outset, she didn't like Dotty. With her bleached brassy blonde hair, thick black roots, and a body that wobbled when she walked, Dotty was surprised to find out she was married. She couldn't understand why Mo sang her husband's praises so much. By the sound of things, he was never home, and he was a gambler. How had she grabbed herself a fella? Who would be interested in a woman with missing teeth at the front? It didn't seem fair somehow to Dotty that she made all this effort with her appearance yet couldn't find a bloke.

Dotty was soon on the receiving end of Mo's interference. Mo kept appearing in Dotty's section, checking up on her. She would have to be careful from now on. The staff all had their own areas, but the borders were blurred. Mo accused Dotty of crossing the line and not being where she was supposed to be. Her pettiness caused friction between the two women.

"Have you taken my duster?" Mo stood in the doorway of the classroom where Dotty was working, her hands on her hips. Luckily, Dotty was a light sleeper and stirred when she heard Mo's footsteps. Thankfully, she was only dozing, so Mo never caught Dotty snoring.

"What do you mean, *your* duster?" Dotty's tone was sharp and defensive.

"I've put my name on everything, so no one can take mine."

"What!" Dotty had never heard such nonsense. The store cupboard where the communal cleaning products were stored held plenty of equipment that were for everyone's use. "You can't do that."

"Oh, yes I can," Mo said with a ripple in her voice. "Mr Morris told me I could. He said it was a good idea. That way they'll be able to see who's nicking stuff." Her tone was accusatory.

"No one's nicking stuff. Who would want to steal disinfectant?"

"You'd be surprised what gets taken from this place. I counted the toilet rolls last week and unless there's been an epidemic of diarrhoea then someone is helping themselves."

"Gosh, how petty." Dotty hadn't noticed anything going missing but then again, she had paid little attention to the bleach and other products. "Anyway, in answer to your question, I haven't had your duster." Dotty had tight hold of a yellow duster and Mo walked over to check, like a mouse sniffing out cheese.

"Let me look." She tried to take the cloth out of Dotty's hand. Dotty was too quick for her and snatched it away.

"Get off, you moron. What are you playing at, coming here accusing me? I'll report you to Jim."

"Don't be so disrespectful, he's Mr Morris to you. I've a good mind to tell him what you called me."

"Go ahead, you petty woman and leave me alone."

"You've not heard the last of this." Mo stamped her feet and marched out of the room. Dotty shook her head. This was worse than the school playground.

Things came to a head a few days later when Dotty was taking another short break. She lay with her head resting on her folded arms on one of the desks. She looked up just in time to catch Mo walking in. Not convinced she hadn't been spotted, Dotty went on the attack immediately.

"What do you want this time?"

"If you were supposed to do the toilets on this floor, you haven't done a good job of them."

"Look, I don't answer to you. If Jim isn't happy with my work, I'll wait and hear it from him."

"Well, I've been to tell him."

"I thought you might. So, what's wrong with the toilets?"

"There's poo down the side of the pan in one of the cubicles in the men's bog."

"That's ridiculous. I cleaned them. Someone must have come in and dumped their load after I left. Anyway, what are you doing checking up on me? That's not in your job description."

"I'll do as I please and you need to speak to Mr Morris about it because I've reported you."

Dotty couldn't believe that only a few weeks back she was having an easy life. Everything seemed fine until Mo's arrival.

"Are you joking? I'm not happy about your behaviour. What happened to teamwork?"

"I'm not very pleased with yours. You're not pulling your weight in this team." Mo stood with her feet apart and her hands on her hips, chewing gum. Dotty thought it felt like a scene from the OK Corral. Mo looked ready to pull something out, not a gun though, probably her tongue.

"It's about time I spoke to Jim about you meddling in everything." Dotty brushed past Mo. She planned to disappear before the posse arrived. She went on the attack in search of her supervisor. When she found him, he was having a coffee break with a fellow cleaner. She asked for a quiet word and told him of her complaint about Mo. Jim Morris just wanted a quiet life. He wanted everyone to get on, but he knew from Mo's moans about Dotty that was unlikely to happen.

"Try to humour her. Her bark is worse than her bite."

"Everything was fine before she started." Dotty marched off, unhappy that Jim didn't take her side.

The final straw came for Dotty a few weeks later when Mo stormed up to her and accused her of taking her mop bucket.

"Why would I do that?"

"You probably did it on purpose." Mo had gone to the trouble of painting her name on many of the items she had acquiesced. In her eyes, they were her own. Dotty had seen and heard enough. She wasn't about to start a war over a mop, so she handed her resignation in that day. The job was tiring anyway. If necessary, she would work extra shifts at the wine bar, but she could no longer stand to be around such small-minded petty people. The cleaning position wasn't that important to her.

Ironically, if she'd have been patient and waited another few weeks, Mo herself was given her marching orders. It turned out that the missing products and equipment had seen its way into the boot of her car. She had been doing a roaring trade, selling the cleaning company's stock off at car boot sales.

## Chapter 16

Rachel and Kylie witnessed Dotty's foul mood that weekend when they met. In Dotty's mind, Mo was an imbecile, and she found it difficult not holding onto a resentment against the woman.

"Let it go," Rachel said. "Be thankful you'll never see her again."

"Did I tell you her husband, Bert works at Devil's Bridge Farm?"

"No. Forget about her, Dotty. You're better just working at the wine bar. You get a better class of clientele there," Rachel said. "Anyway, changing the subject, how's your love life going? Are there any dishy punters you've met while working in that trendy place?"

"My love life is non-existent." Dotty chewed her food. She'd treated herself to a double chocolate chip cookie. Her lower lip protruded. "Kylie's the one getting all the action at the moment."

"I don't know what I've done to deserve someone like Will, but he seems to adore me. He's been very attentive and hasn't put a foot wrong."

"Does that mean Barry is history?" Dotty asked. Kylie had an on-off relationship with Barry that had lasted years. It was as though the two of them couldn't stay apart from each other for long.

"Who?" Kylie laughed as the buttery aroma of the coconut cake wafted tantalisingly under her nose. She closed her eyes and breathed in before taking a bite. She gasped with delight as her teeth sank into the spongy layer, setting her taste buds off singing as the buttercream hit the back of her throat.

"It must be love." Dotty smiled.

"Or at least infatuation," Rachel added.

"He's got it worse than me. He doesn't stop texting me, asking what I'm wearing and telling me what he wants to do to me."

"Don't speak too loudly. There are mothers and children here." Rachel looked over at the next table where three young mums had brought in their babies in prams. As if on cue, one of the tots started to wail. The Strawberry Tea rooms were as busy as ever. If business continued in this vein, the girls may have to take their custom somewhere less noisy, especially if they were discussing intimate or confidential matters. Realistically though, it was unlikely they would go anywhere else. They loved the ambience here, and the cakes were to die for. Dotty and Kylie would need to be prised away from the confectionery using heavy lifting equipment.

"Has Will mentioned anything else about the unfortunate incident at the farm?" Dotty asked as she sipped her mocha coffee and scoffed the last of her chocolate cookie.

"Not really. He doesn't talk much about work."

"Well, don't make us blush by telling us what you do talk about." Dotty smiled.

"You know me too well." Kylie winked. A smear of buttercream seeped out of the corner of her mouth and Dotty signalled for her to lick it up. "That cake was perfection. I must let the staff know." Occasionally, the management allowed them to sample some of their new creations before they were let loose on the public. It was a thank you for the loyalty the three friends had shown towards the café, especially when it changed hands and the sisters took over ownership from their mother. They had even included some vegan products which pleased Rachel.

Dotty listened again to Kylie's encounter about her first meeting with Will. Kylie loved telling the story over and over. The magnetism between them was hard to put into words but she did her best to describe it and how he made her feel. It wasn't just that she had come alive. There was a sense of foreboding. It felt to Kylie like she was going into the unknown which was unusual for a young woman with her experience. She couldn't put her finger on why Will made her feel that way but there was something alluring about his moody charm. It wasn't the fact he rode a motorbike either, that made him seem dark and mysterious. He reeked of danger.

Secretly, Dotty was envious that her friend had found someone. Now, it looked like both her best friends would be hitched before her. If she wasn't careful, she would be left on the shelf. The way her body was hurtling towards her thirties, if she didn't act soon, it would be too late. No one would be interested in a wrinkly old maid. She would be banished to sweeping floors and knitting like she imagined old people did as it was what her gran did. Hopefully, someone would come into her life soon. Maybe she should resort to swiping right on Tinder, although the last time she tried that, it ended in disaster. A guy she hadn't even met became a potential stalker. He wouldn't stop messaging her and it got her worried that there were a bunch of weirdos out there. No, she would stick with the good old-fashioned way of meeting someone at the local nightclub. There were one or two good-looking guys who came into the wine bar, but she was usually too busy serving to talk to them. She sighed. Maybe, she needed to put more effort into this dating game.

Her phone pinged. It was Dave asking if she fancied going to the cinema. He had a night off and wanted to watch the new musical about Elton John's life. She would happily settle for an evening out with her gay friend. All her other friends were partnered up and busy. Even Milly had found someone new. If she wasn't careful, she would start feeling sorry for herself and think there was something wrong with her. What the real issue was, she was too picky, and she made bad choices when she did eventually find someone she was attracted to. No, an evening out listening to Elton's music would be fine. It would be preferable to sitting at home with the family complaining about the lack of anything good on TV.

Later that night, she met Dave. Popcorn in hand, they made their way into the auditorium.

"I'm looking forward to this." He smiled.

"It's better than shovelling up drunks after their late-night revelries." Dotty laughed.

"Yes, I've heard good reviews about it. I'm glad you asked me."

They both enjoyed the film and Dave invited Dotty back to his cottage for a coffee and a nightcap. She felt tired but decided to make the most of her night off. His place was cosy and welcoming, but she felt the décor was more in keeping with a pensioner's style rather than a young copper. She settled down in the comfy armchair with the floral covering. They chatted for a while. Her eyes drooped. She stared into the open fire. It was actually a gas one but looked very authentic, probably made more so by the carved wooden surround and mantelpiece. A gold clock sat centre stage, and she listened as the chimes struck eleven. She should make a move but felt content. Dave was busy chatting away about possible holiday locations for next year.

"I believe Dubai is nice in the spring." He sat with his legs crossed and his finger and thumb under his chin leaning forward.

"Dubai would be great any time of year. Chance would be a fine thing. I'll be happy with two weeks in Spain if I can save enough. The Middle East may be a bit too hot and expensive for me, especially with my pale skin."

"Well, we can dream, and anything is achievable if you put your mind to it."

"Talking of the Middle East, have you made any inroads into finding out who that dead chap is?"

"Funny you should mention that. We have made a possible connection. Currently, we are waiting for someone to come over and identify the body. A woman in Qatar came forward and said she thought it might be her uncle."

"Do you know anything about him?"

"It hasn't been confirmed that it's him yet but the gentleman she thinks it could be is called Mohammed Al Khalifa. We've not got all the intelligence through on him. We're waiting for a positive identification. It's known that Mohammed's bank account hasn't been touched since the date of the accident, so that makes us hopeful."

"Was he working here?"

"He was possibly on business, but we'll pursue more when we get confirmation. The potential named person in question had a healthy bank balance but there probably aren't many poor Arabs." Dotty felt too tired to register this important discovery. Whoever he was, it had nothing to do with her. Her only curiosity was concerning the fact James' lover was also from Qatar. She wondered if she would get a chance to ask him about it, maybe at the soiree coming up that James had planned. Dotty was looking forward to that and checking out his luxury penthouse. She yawned then made her excuses to leave.

# Chapter 17

Rachel had a cunning plan. Whether it was spending so long around Betty Simpson or having a friend like Dotty who couldn't keep from interfering in other people's business, she wasn't sure. Whatever the reason, she was intrigued to find out more about the mystery man found dead at Devil's Bridge Farm. She also wanted to meet Kylie's new fella, Will, but she had an ulterior motive, to sound him out about the man who died. She invited Kylie, Will and Dotty around for a meal at her place. Since Harry from accounts moved in with her, they had splashed out on a new sofa and dining table. She had allowed him to hang up some of the artwork he collected. So, her place looked different. By the weekend, Harry would have finished painting the living room. Two coats of lemon sherbet emulsion and the place would look bright and airy, like a new pin. She couldn't wait to show off her design skills and impress her mates.

"Harry, can you uncork the wine to allow it to breathe?"

"Who's a pretty girl then?" That wasn't Harry. Their new parrot, Pollyanna had started speaking. Harry especially would have to watch his language around the bird. They didn't want her picking up any bad habits. Whatever would their guests think?

"That vegetarian casserole smells good."

"Yes, I'm glad you found the recipe and agreed to try it. I know you're not vegan and you're only eating this stuff to please me, but it will be better for you in the long run."

"Yes, I'm sure. I can just about stomach tomatoes and puy lentils. I hope your friends like it."

"So do I. Could you set the table, please?"

"Set the table, please," the parrot repeated.

Rachel's cookery repertoire was small, and she didn't fancy chancing anything too complicated on her guests. Kylie and Dotty might not mind, they had sampled enough of her disasters in the past, but this was Kylie's new man she was trying to impress. Rachel fussed around, re-arranging the floral display. Her interior design flair was far better than her cooking ability. Harry was good though. He would often nip in the kitchen and test whatever was on the stove. If he felt it needed more seasoning, he would add a few herbs or spices and keep quiet. He didn't mind Rachel taking the glory for whatever they ate. He walked into the kitchen, leaving Rachel in the lounge. Glancing back, he saw her straightening the tablecloth. Quickly, he took the casserole dish out of the oven and tasted it. It needed another stock cube. As quick as a flash he performed his magic on the otherwise bland stew before Rachel noticed.

"What are you doing in there? Come and help me fold these napkins."

"Coming, my love." He smiled. Anyone would think the Queen was coming over for supper, the way Rachel had taken out her Sunday best crockery and cutlery. He walked up behind her, watching her expertly fold the serviette into a fancy looking flower. "That looks terrific." He kissed her cheek and the buzzer sounded.

"Oh no, they're here and I'm not ready."

"Don't panic. I can keep them amused while you finish off everything." Harry was so laid back and couldn't understand why his partner got worked up over the smallest things.

He went to the door to let the guests in. He shook Will's hand and kissed Dotty and Kylie. Will obviously didn't feel he had to dress for the occasion and wore a pair of scruffy jeans with a black jumper and a black leather jacket. He didn't smile but then he rarely smiled. He wore that moody expression that Kylie so loved. After the initial small talk where Harry organised drinks for everyone, Rachel announced that the food was ready. They made their way to the table.

"You've gone to a lot of trouble here, Rachel." Dotty pulled a chair out and sat at the table.

"Oh, it was nothing," Rachel waved her hand. Harry was bemused by her comment and wondered what Dotty would have made of things half an hour ago when Rachel was flapping. Plates of hot food were placed in front of everyone.

"This smells good." Kylie lent forward and breathed in the savoury aroma. She could be relied upon to eat anything and had been on the receiving end of many a burnt offering courtesy of her friend. Rachel was often known to burn toast, so Kylie knew Harry must have had a hand in organising this meal as it was well above Rachel's standards.

"Are you sure you've not got Gordon Ramsay hiding in the kitchen?" Will asked. Kylie winked at him.

"The food is excellent, Rachel." Dotty was surprised. The vegetables weren't overcooked, and nothing was burnt.

"Yes, compliments to the chef." Harry joined in praising Rachel. They ate and chatted.

The plates were cleared away and Rachel handed out plates of shop-bought peanut butter brownies — her culinary skills didn't go as far as making her own dessert. It was then that she veered the conversation to discussing the mystery death at the farm.

"Were you working that day?" she asked Will. His eyes moved in different directions and she watched as a vein pulsated close to his temple.

"Yeah, over the other side of the farm. To be honest, I heard the cattle stampede but didn't think anything of it."

"Did the guy cry out?" All eyes were on Will as they waited for his reply. He looked at his half-eaten brownie.

"Not that I noticed." Kylie frowned at his comment. She thought it was an unlikely response, but she wasn't about to challenge him. For whatever reason, he seemed to be holding something back.

"Who found him?" Dotty asked.

"I believe Ned went over to sort out the cattle. A few of the other lads were probably there. I can't remember."

Now Kylie knew he was definitely lying. This was the biggest incident to hit the area in years, not just the farm. There was no way he would forget the course of events. An accident like that would be engraved on his mind.

He swallowed a spoonful of cake and licked his spoon. With the other hand, he swept his fingers through his hair, looked at Kylie and smiled. Dotty noticed what looked like a smirk. She wondered what he was hiding. The others at the table watched him. If he felt uncomfortable being in the limelight, he didn't show it. There was a silence that was only filled when Dotty's phone rang. She excused herself and rose from the table. She moved into the hall to take the call.

When she walked back into the room, her guests had started up a conversation again. Harry had tactfully changed the subject to ask Kylie about her course. They turned to look at Dotty. She didn't want to interrupt but had some bad news.

"What's the matter, Dotty?" Rachel asked.

"That was Milly. She's in a right state. She couldn't stop crying."

"Why what's happened?" Kylie asked.

"Her new dog has died." Dotty glared at Will.

## Chapter 18

"So, what happened with Tara, your puppy?" Dotty got the full low down off Milly the following day.

"For the first two weeks, she was fine. She ate well, seemed happy, like a normal little dog."

"Then what happened?"

"She started vomiting. I wondered if she had developed a food intolerance. She wasn't keeping any food or water down, so I took her to the vets. He kept her there for ages while he tried to discover what the matter was. Eventually, he said there was no hope, and she needed to be put down. I was shocked and couldn't accept that course of action, so I asked for a second opinion. We found a specialist who said he could insert a feeding tube. It was while Tara was there that they discovered she had a condition affecting her oesophagus which meant food got stuck in her throat. That caused her to be sick. Since that discovery, we'd been pureeing her food and feeding her via a test tube eight times through the day and night. It was hard work, very laborious. The worry was that Tara wasn't putting any weight on. Sadly, the vet wasn't optimistic about her survival." Milly sniffed.

"So, then what?"

"It was heart-breaking. She had lost a lot of weight and was so weak. I had to hold her to feed her like a baby. It turned out she had more conditions wrong with her. There was a problem with her autoimmune system, her bowels weren't functioning normally. In the end, there were so many things the matter, I was advised that the only humane action was to have her put down. I'd have spoken to you sooner, but I know you've been busy."

"Milly, I told you I would always be there for you. You've been unfortunate that you bought a puppy with all those conditions." The only saving grace seemed that the puppy was young and new to Milly, so she hadn't invested too much time and affection on the small animal.

"Well, here's the thing. The vet didn't think it was down to bad luck."

"What do you mean?"

"He thought Tara started life at a puppy farm."

"Forgive my ignorance, but what are the issues with that?"

"Puppies are brought in cheaply from abroad. They have a high risk of disease and aren't well looked after. They are bred purely as a money-making commodity for profit. Because of the conditions they live in, they often have mental as well as physical conditions. The vet told us that this problem is common and a lot of his work with puppies is because of unscrupulous puppy farmers."

"Is there anything that can be done?"

"I could try to sue Ned Bristow, but I've been advised that the chances of winning would be slim."

"That doesn't seem right."

"No, but I can't prove that he is operating illegally. The RSPCA is campaigning for the government to bring in mandatory licensing for anyone selling puppies. That would stop exploitation."

"What are you going to do?"

"I plan to get another dog. I'm not giving up. It's been traumatic and I need time to recover from what happened to Tara. Next time I will go to a rescue centre and not be so eager. It galls me to think of Ned Bristow getting all that money out of me, but I won't make the same mistake twice. I'm sure I can find a good dog to give a loving home to."

"Something should be done about Ned."

"I can't prove he has done anything wrong."

"It doesn't seem right that he can get away with it."

"I know, but I'll just have to put it down to experience."

"I'm so sorry, Milly. You told me you were having issues with Tara, but I didn't realise you were experiencing anything this bad."

"It won't happen again."

Dotty and Milly ended the call. Dotty's head spun. She couldn't imagine what her friend must be going through to lose two dogs so close together. Milly may be happy to put it down to experience, but Dotty hated to think Ned Bristow may have got one over on her friend. She wasn't about to sit back, and watch Milly treated in such a way.

To cheer Milly up, Dotty offered to pop over and give her a free haircut. Milly was delighted. What Dotty failed to mention was that Milly would be a guinea pig and Dotty's first client. Dotty hadn't been let loose on cutting anyone's locks yet. Milly's hair was long and straight, so there wasn't much could go wrong. She would be an easy first model to target.

Dotty arrived with her bag of hairdressing equipment. Milly didn't even look apprehensive.

"You know I'm not qualified yet and I've not had much practice." Dotty couldn't bring herself to tell Milly that she was her first.

"Yes, that's fine. I only want a trim. Half an inch off would be great."

Dotty sat her model down and sectioned the hair off like she'd been shown by her tutor. She slowly and carefully brought each strand down and began cutting. She made the first chop then moved to the other side. As she took a step back, she realised that both sides weren't even. Milly chatted away. She had no idea that Dotty's heart was pounding. As she went to rectify the matter, Milly moved.

"Keep your head still, Milly." Dotty's forehead perspired as she tried to even both sides.

"I trust you implicitly." Milly smiled at Dotty through the bedroom mirror. It was a good job she hadn't focused too closely on Dotty's face and seen the worry lines deepening. Half an inch became an inch. Dotty noticed that if Milly bent her head forward more, it changed the angle of the cut and didn't look right, so she had to lob off some more. The inch became two inches as Dotty rectified her mistake. She stood back and checked the cut again. It wasn't perfect, so another inch came off making it three as Dotty tried to make sure that both sides of the hair were even. The process was painstakingly slow but Dotty reassured Milly it was to ensure her hair was perfect. In truth, if she didn't stop cutting soon, Milly would have no hair left.

Finally, she convinced Milly that she needed to chop so much off to get rid of all the dead ends.

"There, look at that. It looks sensational." Dotty held a mirror up to show Milly the back.

"It's shorter than I expected." Milly gulped and pulled down the hair strands. There was nothing could be done to change it. If Milly was upset, she didn't show it.

"This new shorter style is all the rage. I promise you, that's how all the models are wearing their hair."

"As long as you think it suits me."

"Oh yes, it looks fabulous." Dotty prayed that she had convinced her friend. The whole process took over three hours and caused Dotty no end of stress but at least it took Milly's mind off what happened with her pet.

## Chapter 19

Dotty phoned Kylie and told her the full story about Milly's dog and the resentments she had against Ned. While Kylie was sympathetic, she agreed with Milly and didn't think anything could be done. Dotty was curious to know more. She wouldn't let the matter rest. There was Will to consider. How much did he know about goings-on at the farm? From Dotty's perspective, the jury was out on him. She had a hunch he knew more than he was saying. If Kylie's pillow talk couldn't get anything out of him, then Dotty would have to resort to more drastic measures and tackle him herself. Kylie mentioned that Will was coming over to her place that evening, so Dotty took Winnie out for an early evening walk and they just happened to wander past Kylie's home. She turned up at Kylie's flat unannounced.

Kylie opened the door to Dotty. Winnie barked ferociously when she saw Kylie eating a chip butty. Winnie always preferred chips to dog food, so Kylie gave the dog half of her sandwich.

"Go on then, Winnie. It'll do you more good than me." She smiled at Dotty whose red cheeks glowed from the cold night air.

"It's good to come indoors for a nice warm drink." Dotty hinted, rubbing her cold hands together. "We've had a lovely long walk over the meadow. I thought I'd check if you were in as we were passing." She knew full well that Kylie would be in. Kylie didn't move. Dotty continued, "I wouldn't mind a cuppa if you're putting the kettle on."

"I wasn't but seeing as it's you, I'll organise one. I'm expecting Will any time soon."

"Oh, well, don't let me disturb you."

"No, it's okay. There's something I wanted to talk to you about anyway."

"Oh, what's that then?" Dotty followed Kylie into the kitchen and watched her prepare the drinks.

"It's Candice from college, her behaviour is concerning me."

"What, you mean the way she copies everything you do?"

"You've noticed as well, have you?"

"It's hard not to notice. It's comical. She's even started to sound like you. Her accent has changed. It's most bizarre."

"If it was just my appearance she copied, I might not mind. To be honest, at first, I was flattered that she wanted to look like me but it's becoming obsessive. She's been coming in the pub and telling everyone she's seeing a farmhand. When I asked her about it, she described Will. It spooked me out. I thought he was cheating on me. I tackled them both and made a right fool of myself. He doesn't even know her, and she got tongue-tied when I challenged her about meeting her new fella. I think it's in her imagination."

"I wouldn't worry about it too much. Like you say, it is a form of flattery and the poor girl idolises you. I can't think why." Dotty laughed.

"Oy, you, don't be so cheeky. I'm a good catch. Ask Will." As if on cue, the buzzer to her flat rang. "That'll be him now." Kylie moved over to the mirror and pouted. "I'll do."

"I'll get out of your way." Kylie seemed pleased that Dotty got up to make a move to go. "Come on, Winnie. Let's get your lead. I'll wait and say hi, so it doesn't look like I'm being ignorant."

The doorbell rang and Kylie let Will in, giving him a peck on the cheek as he swept past her into the hall.

"Hi, Dotty." He bent down and stroked Winnie. "Nice dog."

"Hi, yes, we've been for a long walk and were in the area. We're on our way out. Talking of dogs, my friend Milly had a lot of issues with her puppy that died, the one your boss sold to her."

"Yeah, it was a bit of bad luck, that." He wouldn't look Dotty in the eye.

"The vet seemed to think Tara may have come from an unscrupulous puppy farm. Do you know anything about Ned's breeding methods?" Kylie frowned at her friend.

"Nah, he looks after his animals well." He crossed his arms over his chest and still wouldn't look at Dotty.

"Have you worked for him long?" Dotty's eyes narrowed when she asked the question

"A few years, why?"

"Just asking. Anyway, I'm off." Will may not have engaged eye contact with her while she questioned him about the farmer, but she felt his eyes boring into the back of her head as she left. "See you both soon." She wondered what to make of Will's reaction.

A few days later at college, Dotty walked up to grab a coffee whilst on her break from her theory session on nails. She spotted Kylie and James sat in the corner so waved to them and strolled over to join them. They were deep in conversation but stopped chatting to welcome her.

"Hi, how's it going?" Kylie asked.

"I almost didn't recognise you with your new red colour. It suits you."

"Oh, I was a model for the Clynol session and, at the last minute, thought I'd have a change. I know they say that blondes have more fun, but I'm experimenting to see if redheads can enjoy themselves too."

"I'm sure you'll find they can." Dotty laughed. "I still haven't let anyone loose on my hair. The most daring I've been was when I allowed Donna to blow wave it," she said, stroking her hair. "Even then, she didn't do it how I like it."

"I know, it's hard for hairdressers to do it the way you want." James nodded. "The red accentuates the colour of Kylie's eyes, don't you think?" James gazed at Kylie's hair then turned to Dotty.

"Yes, I like it."

Kylie's face glowed. She wasn't someone who went coy when she got a compliment. She loved being around people who gave her favourable comments, the more the better.

"I'm hoping that Candice won't be brave enough to copy this style." Kylie looked across at James and they both raised their eyebrows.

"Have there been more incidents of her copying you?" Dotty asked.

"You could say that. It is getting decidedly weird."

"Why, what has she done now?"

"You know how she came over to my flat the other week?"

"Yes." Dotty nodded.

"She was gushing about how much she liked my furniture. She said she loved my rugs and cushions and all my little knick-knacks." Kylie motioned for James to speak. "Go on, James, you tell her."

"I dropped her off at her home last night after our evening session and she invited me in to see her new purchases. She told me she had been doing her place up, and she wanted a second opinion. She wanted me to tell her what I thought. I was gobsmacked when she opened the door. It was a carbon copy of Kylie's home."

"Oh no, that's awful. What are you going to do about it?"

"I don't know. I mean, what can I do?"

"She doesn't mean any harm, I'm sure, but, sadly, she doesn't have a mind of her own. She's got it bad. She never shuts up talking about you, Kylie." James slurped his drink down.

"That's true, she has put me on a pedestal and I'm the last person anyone should be hero-worshipping. I wouldn't say I was a good role model."

"Yes, if she follows your behaviour, she could get into some serious trouble." Dotty laughed.

"We're joking about it but it's not funny. She likes everything I post on Facebook. The other day I didn't acknowledge something she'd posted, and she got upset with me. I told her I hadn't seen it. It isn't normal to expect my reaction to everything she does. I'd block her, but she'd find out and that would upset her."

"It's a difficult one. If you ask me, the best thing you can do is distance yourself from her. Hopefully, she'll get the message without you having to be cruel."

Dotty nudged James' arm as he spoke. He couldn't see who had walked up behind him. As if on cue, Candice approached their table and asked if she could join them.

"Sure, I'm just leaving," Kylie said. "I need the loo before the next session."

"Wait, I'll come with you." Candice looked hurt by her friend's sudden departure. Dotty grabbed hold of her arm.

"I wanted to ask your opinion on something, Candice. Kylie, I'll catch you later."

"Oh, okay." Candice watched as Kylie and James left them. Her face looked like an abandoned puppy. "What is it you wanted, Dotty?" Candice frowned, put out that she couldn't join Kylie.

"Erm, I wondered if you have a way of remembering the different nail disorders?"

"What are you talking about?"

"We've done the session in our group and I don't know how I will remember the different types. You seem switched on. I wondered if you'd found an easy way to figure out which was which." Candice stared at Dotty, still frowning. It had taken all of Dotty's brain cells to come up with a question to ask Candice. Now she had put it out there, it did seem rather random.

"You wanted to ask me about nail disorders?" Candice's mouth was wide open.

"Yes, that's right. Is it onychauxis where the nail bed parts?" Candice's eyes narrowed.

"No, That's onycholysis. Onychauxis is where the nail thickens."

"Oh, I see, so what's onychoptosis then?"

"Dotty, you need to study them." Candice tutted and shook her head. "That's the one where the nail sheds and onychorrhexis is when you have vertical ridges."

"Oh, great, and do you have an easy way of remembering which is which?"

"No, I don't," Candice sighed. "I learnt and studied them like everyone else."

"Oh, I see, well thank you for clarifying everything. Your hair looks nice, by the way." Candice still had hers blonde with a pink streak at the front, the same as Kylie's was the previous day.

"Thanks. I'm getting fed up with it and thinking of going red."

"No, no I wouldn't do that." Dotty had a tight grip on Candice's arm as though she was about to stop her jumping in front of a train.

"Why ever not?" Candice didn't have a very high opinion of Dotty. She couldn't understand what Kylie saw in this strange being who asked ridiculous questions. Dotty knew it was doubtful that Candice would listen to her remarks, after all in Candice's eyes, Dotty was the enemy, the other woman almost.

"I don't think red would suit your eyes. Your blonde colour makes them sparkle." Candice's eyes weren't sparkling at the moment. They were throwing daggers at Dotty. "Oh, and I hear you've done your place up *exactly* the same as Kylie's." Candice didn't like Dotty's tone or indeed what she might be insinuating. The way Dotty had focused on the word *exactly* riled Candice.

"Are you saying I'm copying Kylie?"

"I'm not saying anything. It's what I've heard."

"Has James been gossiping?" She didn't wait for a reply. "Well, for your information, I haven't done my place out the same, a few things are different. I don't like the way you're accusing me. You're jealous of mine and Kylie's friendship." Before Dotty could answer, Candice had scraped her chair back and stormed out of the café area.

Dotty checked the time. She was due back in the classroom. She sent Kylie a quick text to tell her she had upset Candice. The reply that came back wasn't what she expected.

*Never mind that. There have been some developments around the puppy farming. We need to investigate.*

Dotty was intrigued.

## Chapter 20

Dotty couldn't wait to get hold of Kylie to find out what her message meant. First, she had to listen to the backlash of how she'd upset Candice.

"The poor girl is not a happy bunny. She was outraged when you suggested that she copied me. Doesn't she realise she's doing it?"

"I don't know. It's odd."

"I listened to her moans all through the next session. Even the tutor had to tell her to shut up."

"Oh, dear. Sorry about that. I was only trying to help. What have you found out about the puppy farming?"

"Well, first of all, I spoke to James to see if he knew anything about his dad's business interests, other than general farming stuff. I told him of our suspicions after what happened to Milly's dog."

"Was that wise?"

"Listen, James doesn't have a good word to say about his dad after the way he was disowned. His dad told him he won't be leaving anything to him in his will either."

"I don't think James will be worried about that now he's got his very own Prince Charming."

"No, James' only worry is that if his dad is up to no good, then his mum might be implicated."

"So, what did he tell you?"

"Not a lot. He knows his dad breeds puppies but as he only sees his mum, she isn't aware of all of Ned's business dealings. She keeps out of the way. It's a large farm and they employ people to look after the animals, so his mum doesn't get involved."

"So, what have you found out?"

"I've been crafty, plying Will with drink last night. I couldn't tell you earlier because I didn't want to discuss it in front of James. It's not that I don't trust him, but it is his dad we are suspicious of."

"And what did Will tell you?"

"He didn't go into detail, but he said things are going on at that farm that would make your toes curl."

"Such as what?"

"I don't know. He says he is paid too well to spill the beans on Ned. Apparently, if Ned suspects any of his workers of being disloyal, he doesn't sack them."

"What do you mean?"

"Will said they get roughed up. He explained that working for Ned is like joining the Mafia. Once you're in, there is no way out, you are part of his family."

"Did he indicate what Ned may be up to?"

"No, but I think it involves animals."

"Why, what makes you say that?"

"Oh, it was a comment that Will made when he said it's a good job that he's not a dog lover."

"I see. You're right. We need to investigate this further."

"Do you have any suggestions about how we can do that?"

"Let me sleep on it. We'll come up with a plan by Saturday when we meet up at the café."

Before Dotty walked around to the café the following Saturday morning, there was one person she wanted to visit first to find out if she'd heard anything. She walked up her neighbour's path.

"Dotty, what brings you here this fine morning?"

"Can I come in a minute, Betty?" Betty wasn't dressed. She wore a pink fleece dressing gown and her hair was still in rollers. Thankfully, she had put her false teeth in before she answered the door. She shuffled along in her slippers and Dotty followed her through into the kitchen.

"You must excuse me not dressed yet. I'm normally up and about by now but my back is playing up today. I haven't slept a wink." She stooped as she spoke and rubbed her back.

"Sit down, Betty, if it helps." Dotty helped to ease Betty into her special orthopaedic reclining chair — the one she purchased last summer that all the neighbours had been told about. She told everyone how much it cost her. It was expensive but was much better for her than her previous high-backed chair as it offered extra lumbar support and ease of movement. Plus, the salesman was Gladys' grandson, so it was a no-brainer to buy it. It didn't match the rest of Betty's décor, but she didn't mind if she got relief from the constant pain. Dotty told Betty about what had happened with Milly's dog.

"I knew that man was up to no good. It's an outrage." Betty already had it in for Ned Bristow. She was campaigning for signs to be put up in the area close to the farm to warn of the dangers of cattle. So far, Ned had ignored most of the requests. There was one small notice on his front gate but apart from that there was nothing in the vicinity and Betty didn't think that was enough, given what happened. She started up a petition and planned to march to the council offices unless more was done. She didn't need any more ammunition to nail into Ned's coffin but was still glad for Dotty supplying this extra information.

"I'm trying to find out if anyone else locally has bought a puppy off Ned and had problems with it. I thought you were the best person to come to."

Betty laughed.

"I don't know everything."

"You are the fount of all knowledge in my eyes, Betty. As far as I'm concerned there isn't anyone in the neighbourhood who knows as much as you." Betty was proud of the fact that she was known for being a busybody and a gossip although those wouldn't be the words that she used about herself. She thought of herself as a wise old woman.

"I'm like the Ghigau, the great war women of the Cherokee. I've been reading a love story about one of them."

Dotty's head wandered. In her daydream, she replaced Betty's rollers with a headband and feathers. Her dressing gown was a tribal coat, and she imagined Gladys and Audrey coming over for a pow-wow to speak with their great leader.

Dotty shook her head and brought herself back into the moment.

"Let me know if you hear anything, Betty. I've got to dash. I'm meeting Rachel and Kylie for breakfast at the Strawberry Tea rooms."

"Oh, well, enjoy. I can recommend the buttermilk pancakes or the mixed berry waffles with chocolate sauce."

"Yes, I'm spoilt for choice, Betty. Everything is so scrumptious. I'll be hard pushed to make my mind up."

In the end, Dotty plumped for something savoury — the smashed avocado with poached eggs and zucchini fritters.

"This is to die for," she said as she poked her fritter into an egg and watched the yolk ooze out.

None of the girls could say much while they ate. They were too busy savouring the delights from the kitchen. Finally, Dotty took her serviette and wiped the corners of her mouth. She took a sip of her freshly squeezed orange juice.

"Have you come up with any ideas yet for investigating Ned's puppy business, Kylie? My only hope was to try the wise woman of the Cherokees."

"Sorry?" Kylie looked confused.

"Betty Simpson. That's who she likes to be compared to."

"Oh, I see," Kylie said as she finished the last of her eggs Benedict served with truffles. "That was delicious."

"So, was mine," Rachel added. She went for a lighter but richer option of the chocolate hazelnut croissant.

"I'm trying social media. I've asked if anyone else bought a puppy from Ned's place. Hopefully, others who have had problems with him will get in touch." Kylie poured another cup of tea.

"Is that wise? If Ned gets wind of you going after him, he may not be too pleased." Rachel raised her eyebrows and cocked her head towards her friend.

"Rachel's right, Kylie. From what Will told you, he's got a mean streak. I wouldn't like to get on the wrong side of him."

"Ned Bristow doesn't scare me and as an animal lover it's my duty, plus I can hardly see Ned spending his time on Facebook and Twitter, can you?"

Dotty nodded but inwardly she felt a discomfort that wouldn't go away.

## Chapter 21

"There's a trailer load of bitches coming in from Poland this morning, Will, so get your finger out and look lively. No slouching today, there's work to be done." Ned looked down at the sheet of paper attached to the clipboard he held.

When Will first heard this, he thought it was illegal immigrants being brought in, maybe young women to work on the game. He should have twigged when he opened the back of the trailer and it was full of dogs, tiny puppies to be exact. The smell knocked him back. He stumbled.

"Oh, that stench is bad enough to make me puke." His eyes filled with water. "They smell worse, than you, mate." He looked at his colleague, Anthony who smoked that much dope he constantly stunk of it. It reeked through his pores.

"What do you mean? I *ain't* that bad. I had a shower this morning."

"You've been on the whacky baccy again and it stinks to high heaven, mate but not half as bad as these mongrels." Will insulted the dogs by saying they were mongrels. Ned bought them in good faith that they were pedigrees. He shouted over from the second trailer.

"Shut your mouths, you two and get this motley crew in the outhouse sharpish."

Will lifted out cage after cage of the tiny animals. They were covered in their own excrement and probably had fleas and who knew what.

"We'll need to hose this lot down before we put them in the barn. They're gross." He laid out the cages and turned the water tap on, unravelling the pipe and aiming the hose at the tiny creatures. They yelped out as the freezing water hit their coats. Many of the poor dogs looked scared for their lives.

The noise of the barking sent Anthony more insane than he already was. If his boss hadn't been around, he'd have kicked those bitches for giving him a headache. All he wanted to do was make their lives a misery the same as they were doing to him. He didn't care how cold the water was. He laughed at their reactions. There was a sadistic side to him that made uncomfortable viewing. He was glad he had been brought in on overtime to sort this little lot out. He would get a nice bonus that he could smoke away to his heart's content, out of the way of his partner, Rochelle. She was forever moaning about the amount of pot he smoked every day.

Occasionally, Will shared a joint with him when they were out in the field. Ned drew the line on him smoking on duty, so he had to watch his step. All the cannabis Anthony smoked sent him paranoid and he felt fearful the dogs would escape and bite him. Coming from Poland, he was convinced they would have rabies. The first opportunity he got, he volunteered to go and sort the pigs out, leaving Will to arrange food and water for the litters.

Various breeds had been brought in and they would all have to be catalogued and given straw to sleep on. There would be no luxury items like dog toys and baskets to make them feel at home. Ned saw these animals as pound signs. The sooner they were sold the better. He didn't want to keep feeding them and for them to literally eat away his profits.

There was an assortment of breeds — dachshunds, spaniels and bulldogs. They were all good sellers. He had another shipment due the following week from Ireland, so he needed to turn this lot around and sold off as soon as possible. He was due some terriers, setters, greyhounds and labradors. He already had advance orders for many of the puppies, so he hoped they were well enough to survive the journey.

Ned knew the law was on his side. There was nothing any buyer could do if they were daft enough to buy a sick dog. Once they had signed on the dotted line, they were responsible for the animal's wellbeing. This little lot should bring him in a tidy profit. He would be laughing all the way to the bank.

The hardest part was finding websites and places to sell them from. With the help of the lads, they had various outlets to use. He rarely let anyone come to the farm. It had been a mistake to allow that Milly woman onto his property the other week. It was only because she knew who he was. Usually, potential new owners were met at motorway services and various locations around Sussex using different phone numbers. He didn't want the RSPCA snooping around again. It was bad enough that the Health and Safety Executive had trawled over his land and buildings after the recent situation with the cows trampling that foreigner to death. He had to hire a few extra containers to keep the dogs out of the way until the heat was off the farm. Ned wasn't happy about that.

He knew that his activity was illegal due to the young age of the puppies. He took a risk, but it was worth it for the money it brought in. With the proceeds from that and other ill-gotten gains, he'd been able to buy a brand-new Porsche. He kept it under lock and key and only took it out sporadically. For the most part, he drove around in his battered-up Range Rover. He allowed his wealthy friends and clients a peek at the gleaming red beauty housed in his garage.

"I never knew farming could be so lucrative," Sam Barton stroked the bonnet of the Porsche 911, envious of his friend. He had his own scrap metal business and did okay for himself. They drank together in the Six Bells and he was in awe of his buddy's business acumen. Ned Bristow was a risk-taker and did very well out of it.

Will finished unloading the puppies and moved on to work in the cattle shed. The door creaked open, and he looked up and put his pitchfork down. Ned stood there with his hands on his hips. His face looked like thunder.

"Finish what you're doing in here and come over to my office. I need a word with you." Ned turned and left Will to stew. That sounded ominous. By the tone of his voice and the look on his face, Will didn't think he was getting a pay increase. He racked his brains trying to think what he could have done wrong as he crossed the muddy farmyard a few minutes after Ned left him.

Will knocked on the door to Ned's office and waited. He knew only too well how ferocious Ned's temper could be and he didn't want to give him any ammunition to rub him up the wrong way. It appeared he was already in the doghouse. He waited and knocked again.

"Come in," Ned bellowed. "Sit down." Will looked sheepishly across at his boss.

"What's up?" he asked.

"What's up, what's up!" Ned's fist crashed down onto the desk. He rose from his seating position. His face had gone bright red, and he looked like he was about to have a coronary. Ned paced the floor. "How can you have been so stupid?" He shook his head.

"Why? What have I done?" Will followed Ned's torso as he continued to march up and down the room.

"What have you said to that girlfriend of yours?"

"About what?" Will frowned, dumbfounded.

"Don't give me that. She's on to us and she's asking too many questions. If you don't shut her up, I will. Now, how much have you told her?"

"I haven't said anything, honest."

Ned took Will by the scruff of the neck. He shook the younger man, catching him off guard.

"I've a good mind to stick you in the field and set the cattle on you as well. I don't allow anyone to work for me who's been disloyal."

"Honestly, I've said nothing. You have my word, Mr Bristow. If she knows something, it's not through me."

"Find out what she's got on this place and where she got her information if you want to see your next birthday, that is."

"I will Mr Bristow, I will."

"Now get your backside out of here. I don't want sight of your ugly mush again until you have information for me. Do you get that?"

Will nodded and rushed out the door.

# Chapter 22

Will's head throbbed. What had Kylie done? Why was she snooping around? Had he inadvertently told her more than he intended? He couldn't remember. As much as he tried to think back, he drew a blank. He had so much to drink at Kylie's place that he couldn't recall how the evening ended. He stayed the night and had to shoot off early the following day and he hadn't spoken to her since about the farm. Maybe he hadn't said anything to her? He hoped not, for his sake. He would have to approach this situation with tact.

Kylie was working that evening, so he called in the pub to speak to her. He rarely went in on a Wednesday night, but he needed to know what she knew, and he didn't want to upset his boss. It was imperative he found out what he had told Kylie.

Kylie was pleasantly surprised when Will breezed through the door that night. She smiled and waved to him then went up to serve him as soon as she was free.

"What's up, lover boy? Can't you keep away from me?" Will didn't smile and Kylie picked up on it. "Is anything the matter?"

"No, I've just had a hard day at work."

"Why don't you come back to mine after I've finished, and I'll give you a nice massage." Kylie thought the reason for Will's mood was due to his weary bones. She had no idea that she may be the cause.

"I'll see." He walked off with his pint and Kylie spoke to the back of his head.

"Suit yourself." She pulled a face, then turned to her colleague, Gina. "Men, I don't understand them sometimes."

Will stayed until the end of the evening. He hadn't had time to speak to Kylie as it was busier than usual for midweek. Nursing his pint, he let her get on with what she was doing. He thought about how he would approach the matter of Ned Bristow with her. Another drink would have gone down well, but he purposely didn't want too much alcohol tonight. He needed a clear head and his wits about him when he tackled Kylie. He offered her a lift home, so she was hopeful that his mood had improved when he took her back to her place.

"Come in and take your coat off. Put your feet up and tell me what's wrong." Kylie patted the sofa for Will to sit down next to her. She kept her eyes on his face to see if he mellowed. He didn't speak, but he took her up on the offer of a nightcap. She poured him a brandy. "Come on, what's the long face for? You've been in a foul mood all evening." She sidled up to him on the sofa. "Have I done something wrong?" She wondered if she'd been flirting too much with one of the regulars and Will had got wind of it. Kylie was well known for chatting up men. Her behaviour hadn't stopped because she was seeing Will. It was hard for a leopard to change its spots. He should be grateful that for most of the time she didn't do it blatantly in front of him and that she never went further than harmless chatter.

"I'm in deep water with my boss thanks to you."

"Why? What have I done?"

"He seems to think you're checking up on him."

"After what happened with Milly's puppy, I've got my suspicions about how he is breeding his dogs and I've been making a few inquiries. Surely, you must have seen something?" Will stared at her while he considered what to say.

"You've no firm evidence that he's doing anything untoward, have you?"

"No, but I hoped you could help me on that score."

"Look, I haven't seen anything. Even if I had, I couldn't say because he'd sack me and make sure I didn't get work anywhere in the area. Can I offer you a piece of advice?"

"What's that?"

"Stay away from Ned Bristow. That man is dangerous. He's got a nasty streak and I wouldn't like to see you get hurt. The way you are gunning for him, he's likely to come after you and his ways of silencing people aren't exactly legit."

"Why, what have you seen? What do you know about him?"

"I value my life too much to open my mouth and I hope you feel the same about yours. Trust me when I say, you don't want to go snooping around Devil's Bridge Farm and Ned Bristow."

# Chapter 23

Will stayed the night but was up and out with the dawn chorus. He had to be at the farm just after four, so he left Kylie sleeping. She finally won him over the previous night when she asked him to be a guinea pig to practise the massage strokes that she learnt that day. Knowing her effleurage from her petrissage came in handy when she wanted to work her magic on Will. After a few minutes kneading her palms into his back, he was putty in her hands.

Kylie didn't wake until the alarm on her phone rang. She looked across at the indentation in the pillow where Will had been and smiled. Considering how bad a mood he was in last night it took all her powers of persuasion to win him over. She hadn't lost her touch when it came to seducing men.

Then she remembered what he had said about Ned Bristow and she shuddered. The idea of that bully of a man using Will to warn her off riled her. She went over everything Will said. He knew more than he was letting on. Will might be too scared of Ned to say anymore, but she wouldn't let that brute silence her. It made her more determined than ever to discover what was going on at Devil's Bridge Farm. There was more happening there than she knew already. With Dotty and Rachel's help, they could find out together. Perhaps having another shot at plying Will with drink would do the trick and loosen his tongue. What was that last comment he said about Ned? That Ned had his ways of silencing people.

Will mentioned that Ned's ways were questionable. What had Will seen or heard? A shiver went down her spine as she wondered what he meant.

Thoughts of Ned Bristow were still on her mind as she got ready for college. She needed something to take her mind off him. She had a theory session on the skin this morning and then this afternoon a theatrical makeup practical session to look forward to. Kylie loved working with makeup. She already had a massive toolbox full of every shade of eyeshadow and lipstick because she loved to experiment. The only extra thing she needed to buy for her makeup box was more brushes. She was proud of her collection and knowledge. If she'd been more savvy with her use of the English language, she'd have started up a blog to pass on all she had learnt so far. As her spelling was atrocious, she'd steered clear of that, but James had discussed them setting up a vlog instead and passing on their tips on video. It was something to consider for the future. Right now, she was too busy with work and studying.

The afternoon session at college finished today at 4.30 pm. The way the rotas panned out, they worked late three Thursdays out of four and had started taking clients in as models. This was her week to finish early, so she and Candice had arranged to go into town after college and do some shopping. As much as she thought Candice's behaviour was strange, she was still flattered by the young woman's admiration towards her and they got on well. They had the same sense of humour. The copying hadn't stopped though and Candice messaged her that morning to see what she was wearing. Kylie wanted to lie but that would only upset her friend and deep down she had a soft spot for her and felt sorry for her protege. Her thumbs worked away.

*Not decided yet between my blue jumper and leggings or my new pink jumpsuit. It looks like rain, so I'll probably wear my fawn mac.*

In the end, she chose her blue jumper and leggings for practical reasons. Wearing her jumpsuit was fine until you needed to use the loo. Candice guessed right and turned up in a similar outfit. There may have been a few giggles from the others, but Kylie was thick-skinned enough to ignore the comments.

Candice and Kylie stood in the cloakroom together when they were ready to leave for the day. Candice's fawn mac was similar to Kylie's. It looked new. Kylie hadn't noticed her wearing it before. She decided not to comment. Kylie looked out of the window and saw it had started raining. She took a black beanie hat out of her coat pocket and put it on. When Candice did the same, she sighed.

"Oh, fancy that. I've got a hat like yours." Candice laughed.

"Yes, fancy." As Candice had now also coloured her hair bright red, they looked like twins again. They got the bus into town. The pair of them were busy on their phones and didn't speak much on the journey. Kylie had put another post on social media asking for information from anyone who had bought a dog from Ned. Someone had DM-ed her so she had messaged back asking if she could phone the woman later that evening. Apparently, the woman bought a puppy off Ned and it died. This was an interesting development.

Kylie was still busy scrolling through her phone when they arrived at their stop. The bus was busy, probably due to the bad weather and the proximity to rush hour for the workers. The girls alighted from the vehicle and were herded towards the mall like cattle. Candice was a few feet ahead of Kylie in the small crowd. They shuffled along and waited a few yards up the pavement to cross the road. Everyone watched the traffic passing as they headed to the shopping centre. Kylie glanced up at her friend who was at the front of the group on the edge of the kerb. If Kylie had been concentrating more, she may have seen exactly what happened next. But she was too busy checking her phone at the same time as trying to manoeuvre her umbrella. Constantly looking down when a beep came through became an obsession with her. Because of that, she didn't see what occurred next until it was too late. Her eyes were focused on her mobile and she only looked up when she heard the loud blast of a vehicle horn and screams from the crowd. She raised her eyes in time to watch in horror as a lorry jack-knifed in front of her.

There was a huge commotion. People milled around. She looked all about her for Candice. Panic set in as she couldn't see her friend. More screams rang out and Kylie froze. She pushed towards the front as she took in the sight before her. Through the legs of the people gathered in the road, she saw a body lying on the ground. She gasped and squeezed her eyes shut, unable to comprehend what was there.

Candice lay motionless under the wheels of the lorry.

## Chapter 24

The lorry skidded in the road as he slammed on his brakes. There was no way he could have avoided the collision. The pedestrian stepped off the kerb too quickly. It all happened so suddenly. The driver was in shock. He held onto his grazed head.

"Move out of the way, I'm a nurse," a middle-aged woman with short brown hair shouted whilst parting the crowd. She went over to tend to Candice. Kylie watched open-mouthed as a man and a woman helped the foreign driver out of his vehicle. He looked distressed. Then Kylie's eyes moved over to where her friend lay. She could hardly bear to look. Fear gripped her as she moved closer towards the body lying crumpled in the road. Two women were crouched down in front of Candice and one was giving her CPR. Kylie swallowed as she took in the seriousness of the situation.

"Stand back everyone. Allow some air in," one of the women cried. "Has anyone called the ambulance?"

Four people replied that they had. One man started to control the crowd and ushered people back from the scene. He tried to push Kylie gently away. She leant against his arm which acted as a barrier.

"Let me through. That's my friend lying there."

"I'm so sorry, love." His expression looked grave. He allowed her to pass under his arm.

Others stood by watching, with sadness in their eyes.

"It all happened in an instant. It looks like she's *a-gonna*," an elderly woman with a flat monotone voice said. Kylie scowled at her. The man directing the crowd shepherded people to the corner.

"The police will need to speak to witnesses," he said. "Please don't leave the scene yet."

Kylie looked again at the two women working on Candice. Perspiration poured from the brow of the elder of the pair and they swapped over performing the regimented motions trying to pump Candice's heart. Kylie couldn't bear to watch her friend like this. It only seemed like five minutes ago that they were laughing and chatting on the bus. Now she lay there, her life almost extinguished. Kylie glanced again at the driver. He held tissues over the gash on his head to stem the bleeding.

The police were the first on the scene and took over from the gentleman in charge of crowd control and also the nurse pumping the body. The younger of the two ladies looked pale and shaken. Onlookers who witnessed the tragedy were being comforted by each other and had come together to share their grief. Strangers had arms around each other as it dawned on everyone that Candice was probably dead.

"I've never seen a dead body before," a young man commented. Kylie couldn't bear to look or listen to any more comments. She couldn't get close to Candice now the police had arrived. There was a bench near the entrance of the mall, so she went over and sat down. With her head in her hands, she began to cry. Why couldn't she have been at the front to save her friend? If she hadn't been distracted messing with her phone and putting her umbrella up, could she have saved Candice? A policewoman came across to talk to her.

"It was a tragic accident. There was nothing you could have done." The young policewoman wasn't much older than Kylie. She put an arm around her shoulders to console her. Kylie shivered with the wet and cold. She didn't feel she could be any help to the police. She couldn't even tell them details of Candice's family members.

"Not to worry, we should be able to get her next of kin's details when we access her phone."

"They'll have her emergency contact details at the college." Kylie sobbed.

"Yes, good idea."

Two ambulances arrived together. A few of the witnesses needed treating for shock. A third vehicle arrived, and a paramedic walked over to Kylie. She tried to get up and walk but her legs turned to jelly. She hadn't realised how the impact of what happened could affect her body physically.

"It's okay, take your time. There's no rush." With the help and comfort of the technician's soothing voice, she managed to slow her rapid breathing. Her heart had been racing frantically since the incident and gradually she was able to compose herself and feel more normal again.

She was kept at the scene for an eternity. Candice had been blue-lighted to the hospital.

Kylie wanted to go with her but as she got up to walk towards the ambulance, her legs buckled again. The world around her began to spin, and she fainted. She needed medical help herself to deal with the delayed shock.

She was taken in the ambulance to the hospital with another lady who had hyperventilated and suffered a panic attack at the scene. Kylie came round in the ambulance. It took her a moment to remember what happened.

"Do you think they can save her?" she asked the paramedic.

"They'll do all they can. She's getting the best possible care." Statistically, there was little hope of Candice surviving. They had used a defibrillator at the scene without any success. Theoretically, she had already died twice. It was doubtful her heart would return to a normal state as it had gone into cardiac arrest. The odds were against her, but they never gave up hope until they knew that the brain cells were dead.

Kylie was checked over at the hospital and was allowed to leave. She pushed back the curtain of the cubicle once her observations had been completed. She inquired about her friend. Not being able to get a signal on her phone had caused her more anguish. No one knew yet what had happened, but her priority was to see how Candice was. She rushed up the hospital corridor after finding out where her friend had been taken. As soon as she got close to the ward, it became obvious it was too late. Kylie recognised what must be Candice's sister. She was wailing together with an older woman who turned out to be

Candice's mum. Candice was pronounced dead on the way to hospital.

"I'm so sorry," Kylie said. Her words were unlikely to console the distraught family. "I wish I could have done more, but it all happened so suddenly."

"I can't believe my precious daughter has been run over and killed. After everything I taught her at school to watch what she was doing when she crossed the road. She was probably on that mobile phone of hers. They should be banned." Candice's mum was angry. She wanted to blame someone for her daughter's death.

"I only spoke to her this morning. It seems unbelievable that she is gone. Did you see what happened?" Candice's sister asked Kylie.

"No, not really. Candice was at the front of the group of people waiting to cross the road. As far as I know, she was standing there one minute and the next she was lying on the ground. In this weather, there was no way the driver could stop in time. She must have stepped out in front of him."

"Is the driver okay?"

"I asked the nurse where I was treated. She said he had to have stitches and was in shock, but he has no serious injuries."

"So, no one knows why Candice stepped off the pavement?"

"Not as far as I'm aware."

"Did she seem low? Could she have been feeling suicidal?"

Kylie stared at Anita, Candice's sister and thought for a few moments. There had been no clues with Candice's behaviour to suggest she may do something like that deliberately.

"No, she was happy enough when we decided to go shopping. I don't think that she had any issues," Kylie said. The only problem with Candice was the fact her friend copied everything she did, but she wouldn't mention that.

"Could she have been pushed?" Anita asked. Kylie's mouth opened wide.

"No, that's ludicrous. We've all had a nasty shock. It was a tragic accident. People don't get pushed in front of lorries for no reason."

Kylie lay there that night unable to sleep, trying to rationalise what happened. She went over in her head all their conversations to look for clues to Candice's state of mine. Her stomach churned as she considered the last thing Anita had said — *could she have been pushed?*

# Chapter 25

The tears continued for Kylie as she reflected on recent events. Her mum came to see her together with Rachel and Dotty.

"Some shopping trip that turned out to be. I feel so guilty." Dotty kissed Kylie on the cheek.

"You were a good friend to Candice and did all you could. You weren't to know what would happen."

"Her sister suggested it could have been suicide or worse. She suggested Candice may have been pushed."

"How awful." Rachel put a hand over her mouth. "I'm sure that wasn't the case." The girls looked at each other.

The mood at college was more sombre as the news of Candice's death filtered through. Kylie sat with Dotty and James on their lunch break.

"I still can't believe she's not going to walk in looking like you, Kylie." James patted Kylie's hand.

"It's very sad, and it makes you realise how fragile life is. We could all go in an instant." Dotty clicked her fingers. "One minute she was here talking to us and then puff, she's gone." Dotty shook her head.

"I think we ought to do something in Candice's honour. We must find out if her family have anything planned. It's such an awful waste of a life." James shook his head. "Which reminds me, the soiree is arranged for next week for Khalid's birthday. You're both invited of course. I hope you're going to be able to come, Kylie."

"That would be nice, James." Kylie clapped her hands together. She was dying to meet the rich prince that James talked about all the time. It might help her deal with her grief if she felt up to going.

"Can I bring Will?" Kylie asked.

"If you must, darling. I don't want him getting drunk and letting the side down. Khalid already believes that most Westerners are uncouth."

"He's not wrong there then." Kylie smiled. "Will only gets drunk when I ply him with liquor. He can behave himself; I promise. It's me you need to watch out for."

"You can say that again." Dotty winked at her friend.

Both girls were looking forward to meeting royalty. They had never mixed in such high echelons of society before. They spoke about it when they were alone.

"You never know, Khalid may have a rich straight friend for you, Dotty."

"I doubt it, plus I don't think I could fit in with an Arab's way of life."

"Oh, gosh, yes, you'd have to ride a camel and wear a burka. You're right. I can't see you doing that not for any amount of oil money."

"That's true. Those camels are smelly and why would I want to hide this voluptuous body?" Dotty laughed as she stroked her fingers down the sides of her torso. Secretly, she often detested her body. Her attempt at a sarcastic joke had fallen flat.

"Do we have to curtsey in front of Khalid when we meet him?" Kylie asked.

"I don't know. We'll have to ask James."

By the time the party came around, Kylie was glad of some light relief away from the aftermath of the accident. She was sick of retelling the story, plus when she mentioned it to anyone, she got a knot in her stomach. She wasn't sure if it was regret that she should have done more or fear over what could potentially have been. Will hadn't done much to console her. Every time she tried to speak about the incident, he changed the subject, saying it wasn't healthy to keep talking about it.

Today, she was grateful she could forget about it. She was looking forward to seeing James' fabulous home. Sadly, Rachel and Harry were unable to attend as Harry's nan was ill.

"You'll have to tell me all about it when I see you," she said.

"We'll be going around snapping photos like we're estate agents." Kylie laughed.

The girls and Will arrived at the penthouse apartment thirty minutes late. At the last minute, Dotty had finally chosen to wear a vintage-style A-line retro dress with a lace overlay. Kylie had to help her fasten it. It was an electric blue colour, and she looked stunning. She had put her hair up in the style of Audrey Hepburn and copied her same glamourous signature eyeliner look. Kylie wore her favourite Coast dress, the one she only brought out on special occasions. It was pink satin with a large waistband and full skater skirt.

Will complimented the girls on their appearance. Kylie raised her eyebrows. It wasn't like him to pay her a compliment, but she wouldn't question it. The three of them stood at James and Khalid's door waiting. They heard the loud music coming from inside.

"I hope they've invited the neighbours, so they don't get any complaints," Dotty commented. They were shown into the large split-level lounge. Neon lights flashed like multi-coloured police sirens. A DJ stood in one corner of the room wearing headphones, his head bobbed up and down with the beat.

The girls had clubbed together to buy Khalid a cashmere scarf. It was hard to know what to buy the man who had everything. Dotty had chosen expensive gold wrapping paper and ribbon as she wanted to leave an impression. She held the present tightly in her hand as she manoeuvred out of the sleeves of her coat. They placed their outer garments in one of the spare bedrooms.

"Wow, look at that," Kylie said picking up an ornate gold figurine.

"Put it down, Kylie. It's probably worth a fortune," Dotty whispered. They scanned the large room, deep in admiration of the tasteful décor. Kylie swooned with delight.

"Oh, I could live here. I wonder if they'd like a lodger?" Kylie ran her fingers over the satin throw on the bed. The room was tastefully done out in soft greys and silvers to create a luxurious sparkly feel. A huge modern chandelier dangled over the bed. Kylie's feet sunk into the plush grey carpet. Dotty was already admiring the modern artwork on the walls.

"If this is the spare bedroom, I wonder what the rest of the house is like?" Dotty said, taking everything in.

Kylie took a running jump and threw herself into the centre of the bed.

"Kylie, what are you doing?"

"Sorry, I couldn't resist." She got off the bed and straightened the duvet cover and throw.

"James will have your guts for garters if he sees what you've done."

"Come on, let's find James and Khalid. I can't wait to be shown around. It's magical. James is so lucky having a place like this. It makes my home look like a shoebox."

"Well, we can dream and enjoy the moment."

They walked out and past numerous men getting cosy with each other. Kylie did what she did best and that was to mingle. She worked the room with style leaving Will on his own. He started talking to a chap to his right who turned out to be a police superintendent, something Will didn't feel at ease with. Dotty found a guy stood on his own to chat to. She felt sorry for him being alone but when she found out he was a barrister, she thought that maybe he wasn't as lonely as she suspected.

The friends circled the floor, talking and meeting new people. Dotty and Kylie met up again near the kitchen. They intended topping up their glasses, but Kylie spotted a waiter with a tray of drinks and without asking, helped herself and started necking champagne.

"Do you think there will be anyone else here who's straight? I mean some of these guys are drop-dead gorgeous." Dotty confided in her friend.

"Expect them to be gay then if they're not, take it as a bonus. For now, just look and admire."

"Dave would have loved this party. Let me get you a top-up." Dotty noticed that Kylie had already emptied her glass. "I'll bring it out. You mustn't neglect Will."

"Oh, he's okay. He's talking to some posh chief of police. There are a lot of high-profile people here tonight. I've already rubbed shoulders with a heart consultant and an MP."

"Mind your language and you'll be okay. I'll get you some more Prosecco seeing as you downed that one so quickly," Dotty said, mesmerised at how fast Kylie had greedily guzzled the champagne.

She left Kylie and headed for the kitchen to the drinks. It took her longer than expected. A few of the guys stopped her on the way, starting up polite conversations. One of them commented on her resemblance to Audrey Hepburn, which sent her into a fit of giggles as Audrey was her style icon. After discussing some of Audrey's best films, she excused herself and moved towards the drinks area. She smiled as she passed two waiters serving canapes on a silver tray. This was the life. When she walked into the kitchen, she wasn't surprised to see a special bar set up with a cocktail waiter on hand. There was a long queue waiting to be served, so she decided to crack open one of the bottles of Prosecco they brought with them.

"Oh, you've got a drink." James stumbled into Dotty, touching her shoulder.

"Yes, thanks."

"I'll give you a tour of the place when I get a minute but first you must come and say hello to Khalid," he shouted above the music.

"I'll go and find Kylie and Will. They'll want to see the tour and meet Khalid."

She made her way through the hall to the lounge. There was a bottleneck by the door, and she had to push through to get past.

"Excuse me, drinks coming through," she shouted. She couldn't see Kylie but there was a line of people with their backs to her, cheering loudly. She sneaked up behind one of the shorter guys and stood on her tiptoes to see what they were staring at. She couldn't believe her eyes. Kylie had organised a wheelbarrow race across the vast expanse of flooring. The judge and the MP took part along with a model and a lawyer. Dotty shook her head. It was impossible to leave Kylie for five minutes. If she was like this sober, what would she do with a few more drinks down her? There was raucous laughter as a large black woman with her smaller female partner won the race.

"Having fun?" Dotty asked her friend, as she passed her a drink.

"I had to liven this party up somehow." Will followed her around like a sheep.

"James is going to give us a tour and we'll meet Khalid."

"Come on, Will," Kylie beckoned as her trusty companion followed.

Dotty found James, and he took her hand and led her through into a large drawing room. Kylie followed with Will close behind.

"Great party," Kylie called out to James. The music made her skin tingle. Hazy chatter mingled in the background over the music. James guided Dotty over towards a white grand piano that took pride of place in the lower section of the room.

"Do you play?" Dotty asked James.

"No, Khalid's the wonder boy. He can do anything. He is an expert in any field you name from playing instruments to playing polo, no one can match him," James said as he stuck his chest out with pride.

Dotty passed the present over to the tall handsome prince who was gracious in his acceptance.

"Oh, this is so beautiful. You shouldn't have gone to all this trouble." He held the scarf against his cheek. His dark brown eyes smiled as he stroked it against his trimmed beard. He passed it to James. "Feel the quality, James, dear. I so love cashmere."

Will had been stood in the background and Kylie brought him into the circle.

"This is my boyfriend, Will."

They shook hands then James added, "Will works at Devil's Bridge Farm where that tragic accident happened."

Suddenly, Khalid's face changed. His smile disappeared. His nostrils flared. There was something about his expression that disturbed Dotty. Within seconds, someone else grabbed his attention, and he moved on to speak to them.

When Dotty got a minute alone with Kylie, she whispered in her ear. "What did you make of that? Did you see Khalid's expression when he was introduced to Will? It was most odd." She nodded, deep in thought. The two friends looked at each other, eyebrows raised. What was that about?

## Chapter 26

Kylie had drunk too much Prosecco. At the end of the party, the three friends left together. Dotty and Will held Kylie up to steady her. They helped her into a waiting taxi. After they dropped Dotty off at home, Kylie started on Will.

"Have you met Khalid before?"

"No, of course not."

"Did you see the way he looked at you when I mentioned where you worked?"

"Perhaps he thinks a lowly farmhand shouldn't be attending one of his parties."

"Don't be silly. That wasn't the reason. He seemed okay at first until I mentioned Devil's Bridge Farm."

"Exactly, he thinks I'm less than. I can't stand people like him who look down their noses at the likes of us."

"Don't include me in that. Khalid was nice to me."

"So, you think you're better than me as well, do you?"

"I didn't mean that. If you've got an inferiority complex, it's not my fault."

"Well, you are mates with his lover. He's not going to snub you as he did me. They're all the same, his sort. He's only interested in mixing with people who are from the upper class or have money."

"Rubbish. No, it wasn't that. The way he looked at you, I wouldn't be surprised if he knew that fella who died. I mean they both came from Qatar. You've got to admit, that's a coincidence."

"Leave it out, Kylie. Now, it's you who's talking rubbish. If he knew the bloke, I'm sure he would have said."

"There's more to this than meets the eye. I'd put money on the fact that Khalid knew the dead man, especially after his reaction."

"I've told you before, Kylie, don't get involved. If you carry on like this, we're going to fall out over this." Will shunted along the seat as far as he could away from Kylie. He folded his arms. The poor taxi driver must have wondered if he would have to step in and split up the two lovers as their voices grew louder.

"I'm sick of you telling me what to do. You don't own me, Will." By now the conversation had become heated. Kylie wouldn't let it drop. By the time they arrived outside Kylie's place, the couple weren't speaking.

"I'm not coming in. I've got an early start tomorrow. If you won't take any notice of what I'm saying, then you and I are finished."

"I'm not having you giving me ultimatums," Will replied with a string of expletives. "Well, if that's how you feel." Kylie climbed out of the car without kissing Will or saying goodbye. She kept the money Dotty had given her for the fare and marched up to her front door. Will didn't try to stop her. He told the taxi to drive off. Kylie was in floods of tears as she watched him disappear up the road.

When Kylie woke the following morning, she groaned when she turned towards the pillow beside her and remembered what happened the previous evening. Kylie's head was doubly sore, pounding from the hangover and reeling over what Will said. She'd had time to dwell on his words, in bed alone. She didn't take kindly to anyone telling her what she could and couldn't do. She knew it wasn't wise to go to bed on an argument and this morning was a prime reason why not. Her anger towards Will grew. How dare he drive off like that. She expected him to run up to her and say sorry. It seemed that he was as stubborn as she was. His behaviour made her more determined than ever to find out the true nature of what was going on at Devil's Bridge Farm. No one would frighten her off that easily. Will was in the wrong to speak to her the way he had. She didn't like men who were controlling. He hadn't messaged her this morning like he usually did when they didn't see each other, but she wouldn't suck up to him. She would make him stew. Kylie dug her heels in if she felt she wasn't being treated right.

She needed to tell Dotty what happened between her and Will. She couldn't wait until they spoke together at college the following day. She rang her friend. Whatever Dotty's plans for the day were, they would have to wait until Kylie had finished moaning about Will. She had to offload her woes.

Dotty had her own concerns to worry about. Thankfully, she'd paced herself the night before with the amount she drunk so wasn't suffering as a consequence of the party. She loved being introduced to James and Khalid's friends and was in awe of their apartment. Her head took off wondering what it would be like if she met a prince. She would love to be a princess in a palace. She thought about the staff she would have — a butler to pour her tea, a maid to comb her hair, and a PA to organise her busy social calendar. She picked up the rolling pin she'd been using and placed it on the side while she toyed with the idea of getting a cook when she was wealthy. It was doubtful as she enjoyed cooking so much herself but then being a princess would be a busy job. Ah well, she sighed, returning to the task in hand of making bread. She loved being alone in the kitchen. Her dad was out playing golf and her mum was upstairs changing the beds. Suddenly, her phone rang. She wondered if it was Kylie again, having another moan about Will. It was Dave this time. Her hands were covered in flour and her forehead was sweating with perspiration from kneading the dough. She wiped her hands on her apron, turned the radio she'd been listening to down and answered. Dave told her he had some disturbing news. She sat at the kitchen table to listen.

"Dotty, I don't want you to be alarmed but…" Already Dotty's heart was beating fast with those opening remarks.

"What is it, Dave?"

"This is confidential information that I shouldn't be passing on to you but there's something you ought to know." Dotty breathed deeply. She wondered what her friend had done.

"You promise you won't breathe a word of this."

"I promise."

"I'm not even convinced that Kylie should be told. It could make her worried."

Dave paused for a few moments before he spoke. Dotty waited with bated breath.

"What is it, Dave?"

## Chapter 27

Dave cleared his throat. Dotty could hear his heavy breathing down the phone.

"There was a witness at the scene of Candice's tragic accident that says he saw someone push her."

"You're joking."

"I'm not. The problem is the witness is hardly reliable. He is only a young ten-year-old boy. No one else seems to have seen anything other than…"

"Go on."

"A woman has come forward saying she saw a man running away from the scene."

"So that could corroborate the boy's story."

"The police are keeping an open mind and of course it will depend on what comes out at the inquest. I believe one of the pedestrians took some photographs of the accident, so the police will be studying those."

"Could I look at them? It might help jog my memory with anything I saw."

"Good idea, I'll get hold of them to show you."

"Something has dawned on me and it's sent a shiver down my spine."

"What's that?"

"Kylie was threatened by Ned Bristow through Will."

"You told me he wasn't too keen on her meddling into his business over the dog breeding. Why what about it?"

"If I'm not mistaken Candice and Kylie wore the same clothes that day."

"What are you implying?"

"Well, you know how similar those two looked, how everyone called them twins?"

"Yes, you told me. You don't think it was a case of mistaken identity and if the so-called accident was deliberate that Kylie was the intended victim?"

"I don't know, Dave but it's a worry. If that is the case, then it's even worse news for Kylie. Can you see what your colleagues make of my theory? Kylie may need protection."

"I can put it to them, but they don't work on supposition, just facts. Right now, there is no proof anything untoward happened to Candice or that Kylie life is being threatened."

"I hope Kylie's safe. I would hate to think her life could be in danger. I must tell her, Dave. She needs to be extra vigilant just in case. I'd never forgive myself if I kept quiet and something happened to her."

"Do you think it's wise to say anything? You could be worrying her unnecessarily."

"Wouldn't you want to know if it was you?"

"Probably."

"There you go then. I'll have to tell her about what the young boy said and my fears. She can make her own mind up."

"Okay, but as I say, don't go gossiping about it. The police are still investigating."

Dotty felt numb when she ended the call with Dave and almost jumped out of her skin when it rang straightaway and it was Kylie again. Kylie often phoned back straight after she'd spoken to Dotty with an afterthought. She had been dwelling on the previous night's fall out with Will.

"My head won't shut up. What if he doesn't want to see me again?"

"If he doesn't, then he wasn't the right one for you anyway." Dotty struggled to console her friend. She wondered how long Kylie could survive without hearing from Will. Dotty listened for a while as her friend recounted the same tale that she told her a couple of hours earlier. Now she had time to stew, she wanted to rant some more about her uncaring boyfriend. Dotty was about to make Kylie's problems a whole lot worse. She had to tell her the news. Poor Kylie's altercation sank into insignificance when Dotty recounted Dave's news and she put two and two together. It dawned on her that Ned Bristow may be doing more than just threatening her.

"What am I going to do, Dotty?"

"The first thing you can to do is to pack your stuff and get ready for a short break away. It's my brother's twenty-first birthday next weekend and I said I would go to Manchester to stay with him. You can come too. There'll be non-stop partying."

"Won't the crowd be a bit young for us?"

"When have I ever known you turn down a party? It will make Will jealous if he knows you are mixing with some young studs."

"You're right. I think it's a jolly good idea under the circumstances and a few days away will do me good. It will take the pressure off and allow me to forget about everything that's happened. Thanks for asking, Dotty."

"You didn't think I would go on my own, did you?"

The girls skived off college early on Friday afternoon and Dotty drove the two-hundred-mile trip up to Manchester. Her car was loaded with gifts from family members for Joe. The friends set off in good humour.

"I've bought him a jumper. I hope he likes it."

"You didn't need to buy him anything, Kylie. I'm sure he's not expecting a present."

"You're only twenty-one once and it's the least I can do. I mean, he's putting us up, isn't he?"

"Yes, but we're only on camp beds if we're lucky. If his other mates grab them first, then we'll be on the floor. A few of his friends from school are going but they've booked the train. They could have come with us but there's too many of them."

"They're not all staying with Joe, are they?"

"I hope not. We won't get any sleep if they are."

"I doubt we'll do much sleeping this weekend. It's party time." Kylie started waving her arms and gyrating her body in the seat as she moved in time with the music on the radio.

The journey took an hour longer than they'd anticipated. Rush hour traffic and roadworks hindered their progress.

"Message Joe for me and tell him we're running late. We can always meet him in the pub if he tells us where."

Dotty wasn't the fastest of drivers. By the time they arrived on the outskirts of Manchester, she was shattered. Joe and his mates had already gone out for drinks. He left a key for Dotty under the mat. The girls quickly got changed and touched up their makeup. There was no time to dawdle. Tonight, they would get to meet Joe's friends. Tomorrow was the big party night.

It didn't take Kylie and Dotty long to transform their looks. With a change of outfit, a squirt of hairspray, a smidgeon of lippy and the application of false lashes, they were soon ready to go. Dotty would have liked longer to get ready, but Kylie badgered her to hurry up. She needed a drink. She still wasn't speaking to Will, and she wanted to block out everything that had happened. Oblivion was what she planned for tonight.

They walked in the bar in Didsbury village and the warmth hit them straightaway. Everyone was laughing and joking. Joe had a crowd of about ten friends around him.

"Here, she is, big sis. Come here, Dotty." The siblings kissed.

"Good to see you, Joe."

"How are you, Kylie?"

"Don't ask her that, just get the drinks in. It's thirsty work all that travelling," Dotty said, and everyone laughed.

"You two haven't changed. Always up for a good time." Joe danced with Kylie. He was on his way to getting merry. After the introductions, they found a table to sit down. Dotty was bushed after the long drive. Joe and two of his mates joined them. Before long, their girlfriends arrived and there was a real party buzz about the place. The booze flowed, and everyone was enjoying themselves. If this was the warm-up, what would tomorrow night's party be like?

They were chatting away when Dotty noticed a guy at the bar talking to a friend. He wasn't the usual sort of guy she fantasised about. He had short brown hair, a small nose and dimples and reminded her of Justin Timberlake. She watched him across the crowded bar. He hadn't noticed her, but she was about to change that.

"It's my round. What's everyone having?" she asked to a roar of applause. She knew exactly which part of the bar she would make her way towards. As she approached the handsome stranger, she noticed that he was eating a plate of chips and dipping them in tomato sauce. That wasn't something Dotty was accustomed to but when she got closer to the bar, he turned and held out a chip for her to try. Her legs turned to jelly as she took the greasy French fry off him.

"Come on, don't be shy. Take more than that." He held another chip in his hand as she opened her mouth. He fed her, staring into her eyes. It was the most erotic action she had experienced, and from a handsome stranger at that.

"My name's Robin. Where have you been all my life?" he said, smiling.

Dotty wanted to say some quip back like she'd be his Batgirl any day, but she was struck dumbfounded. Her mouth chewed slowly on the fried potato.

## Chapter 28

Robin put his arm around Dotty's shoulder. The touch was electric. Dotty lit up inside like a Christmas tree. She smiled. If anyone else had done that, she'd have shrugged them off, but she was happy for this handsome guy to be as tactile as he wanted. He peered down into her eyes from his lofty height, all six feet three of him.

"You don't sound like you're from round these parts," he said.

"No, I live in Sussex. I'm here for my brother Joe's twenty-first. He's at Manchester University."

"So, it's my lucky day bumping into you."

"Or maybe mine." Dotty raised one eyebrow. She was normally coy when it came to expressing her feelings, but her voice had set off speaking all on its own. With a gentle touch, Robin scrolled his finger through Dotty's hair and over her cheek.

"What beautiful hair and skin you have." He could not take his gaze off her nor she off him. At that moment, she wanted to push the usual dating protocol aside and kiss him passionately. Instead, she took a step backwards. She was unable to trust her body.

"I better take these drinks back. That lot will lynch me if I take too long." She smiled and disappeared from his side. She felt his eyes boring into her back as she waited for the onslaught from her crowd.

"Where have you been with those drinks? I'm spitting feathers." Dotty didn't reply. She glanced back across the busy bar, catching Robin's attention, and smiled. He stared back at her. Kylie followed Dotty's gaze.

"Oh, I see. It's like that, is it? You didn't waste any time."

"Isn't he gorgeous?" Kylie nodded and Dotty had to tear herself away from looking. She was soon back in with her brother's mates, joining in with the laughing and joking. When it was time for another round, Dotty volunteered to go to the bar again. Foolishly, the others let her. This time, one of the boys had to come and get the drinks off her. She was locked into Robin's side and couldn't pull herself away. She was like iron filings to a magnet. It wasn't just his looks she found attractive but his personality as well. They spoke about anything and everything. He seemed knowledgeable about most subjects. Dotty felt lightheaded with emotion. Something stirred in her that she hadn't felt for a long time. By the end of the evening, she felt like Robin was an old friend she had known for a lifetime. His mate, Phil joined in with their conversation at first but soon realised he was playing gooseberry after spotting the chemistry between the pair, so he left them to it.

At the end of the night, Robin grabbed Dotty by the waist. He pulled her in towards his chest. A small but teasing smile crept over her face. She felt her skin tingle as goosebumps appeared on her torso. Her heart skipped a beat at the anticipation of what she hoped was to come. His lips brushed hers. She wanted to pull away, to take back control, but she was lost, putty in his hands. Her senses were seduced and there was no way back. He took her head in his hands and kissed her passionately. It began slow and soft, building into a crescendo to a hot and fiery embrace. She ran her fingers down his spine, wanting the moment to last forever.

Eventually, she was able to prise herself away, and she invited Robin to Joe's party the following evening.

"How could I say no?" Robin's smile was infectious. It lit up not just his face but anyone else's he encountered. "I'll look forward to seeing you tomorrow, Dotty."

Dotty had a wonderful time at the party getting to know Robin. He told her he had two brothers and lived at home with his dad after moving out from a failed relationship six months earlier. He worked as an electrician. By the end of the night, Dotty was smitten. The party was a great success. Joe loved being the centre of attention. He enjoyed all the presents that were bestowed upon him. Being the birthday boy put him well and truly into the limelight, a spot he relished. Everyone had a great time.

Sunday felt flat by comparison. When Dotty rose from her sleeping bag, there were bodies sprawled across Joe's front room. Only a couple of them stirred before noon. They mucked in to make tea and toast for the other revellers. Before she left for the long journey home, Robin sent through two text messages wishing her a safe journey and that he hoped he could see her again soon. He was all she talked about on the trip back down south. Kylie was half asleep, nursing the remnants of a hangover. She yawned as she slunk down in the car seat.

"So, will you see him again?"

"I hope so. He says he wants to come down to see me, but you never know. He lives such a long way away. It will probably be like a holiday romance where you agree to get together but then reality sets in." She sighed. "Life takes over and soon, you're forgotten about and it fizzles out."

Dotty couldn't have been more wrong. When she got back, she messaged Robin. They contacted each other every day and he arranged to come and see her. Kylie offered to put him up.

"I can't wait to see him again." Dotty smiled as she took a sip of her coffee. She sat with Kylie and James on her break at college later that week.

"Somebody, throw a bucket of water over her." Kylie shook her head. She had patched things up with Will. He didn't get in touch while she was away, so she finally reneged and contacted him. If he wasn't going to apologise, then she would have to be the bigger person as she didn't want to stop seeing him.

"You'll have to introduce me to Robin when he comes down. Khalid and I would love to meet him. We could go out with our respective partners for a nice meal or something." James sat filing his nails.

"Does Khalid do Nando's?"

"Of course, he does." James laughed.

"I would have thought he'd only be into fine dining."

"No, not at all. We do go out to some nice restaurants, and he sneaks to Burger King when no one's watching for a whopper!"

"I thought you could give him that." Kylie winked, and they laughed. "It would be great to meet up and get to know Khalid better, that's if he and Will get on. Did you see how frosty the pair seemed the last time they met?"

"Yes, I noticed that. I asked Khalid what the problem was, but he went silent on me."

"So, he's not admitting to knowing the man who died then?" Dotty asked.

"No, he's not but then it's like when we go to America, everyone asks if we know the Queen. It's ludicrous of course to expect that just because they came from the same country, that they'd know each other."

"It wasn't just that though, James. It was the way Khalid and Will looked at each other. There was a knowing glance between them, I'm convinced of it. There is more to this that we don't know about. We should try to investigate."

"You're right, Dotty. I've got a hunch that Khalid knows more than he's saying. There was something about his body language when I tackled him. He didn't look comfortable.

"And what about you, Dotty? What are your plans?" Kylie asked.

"It's time Winnie and I took a walk to James' dad's farm to check out what is going on there."

"You be careful. My dad is a mean so-and-so."

Dotty nodded, not sure what she was getting herself into but curious to find out.

## Chapter 29

The investigations didn't go well. James and Khalid had a fallout and weren't on speaking terms. Khalid went on the defensive when asked whether he had met Will before the party.

"Of course not." Khalid avoided eye contact and James knew he was lying. "Why don't you believe anything I say. I'm not happy with the way you question me. I love you James and I only have your best interests at heart."

"Then, why can't you be honest with me?" Khalid went into one of his tantrums caused by James' constant questioning. He was due to fly out to Paris that night on business. Things were still frosty between the pair.

"Have a good trip," James said. His voice wasn't convincing. He sat sulking over by the piano when Khalid walked over to kiss him goodbye.

"I will and you've got to start trusting me more." Khalid gave James a peck on the cheek then rushed out to his waiting taxi, slamming the door behind him. It left James scowling, wondering about the state of their relationship.

James had always trusted Khalid even though he was away a lot. Because James was showered with gifts every time Khalid returned, he never questioned what he got up to, but this was different. It didn't take a blind man to see Khalid's discomfort when Devil's Bridge Farm was mentioned.

James did something that he had never been tempted to do during their time together. He went into the room Khalid used as an office and pulled on the desk drawer. It was locked. He took a pin and began working the lock. If he managed to open it, he would blame the cleaner. He probably hadn't thought things through, but he had to look for evidence of any impropriety. His hands shook, and he kept turning around to check the door as if Khalid was going to barge back in and catch him in the act. He eventually forced the lock open. The drawer was full of paperwork that he rifled through. Most of it seemed inconsequential, and there was nothing that immediately jumped out at him. However, the fact Khalid kept the drawer locked made James determined to go through everything with a fine-tooth comb. He had twenty-four hours until Khalid returned.

He sifted and sorted through documents, some of which were in Arabic. He put everything into three piles. One he wasn't interested in, the second for closer scrutiny and the final one was where he couldn't make sense of what was written due to the foreign language. He wondered if this was the pile to focus on. His hands shook as he considered the implications if Khalid found out what he had done. James justified his actions because he never hid anything from Khalid, so why should his partner have secrets from him. James was an open book and had told his lover everything about his upbringing. Khalid wasn't so forthcoming with details of his past. James had always thought it was because of his position. He had to take care of how much he revealed. He knew full well that if anything went wrong between them, unscrupulous souls might reveal what they knew to the Press. Because of that fact, James never pushed Khalid to open up to him. He thought his handsome prince would tell him when he was good and ready. For now, there was mystery shrouding the man.

James held up a bank statement. Khalid had never discussed how wealthy he was. James thought that was because the very rich didn't need to brag about it. When James saw how much was in Khalid's account, he whistled. He could not imagine anyone having so much money. Seeing the sum in black and white made him less worried about his lover buying gifts for him. As James put his hand in the drawer to return some of the papers, he felt something at the back. His fingers touched a solid mass. It was too far back to see what it was but as he pulled it forward, he realised it was a mobile phone. James felt sick with nerves. Why did Khalid hide a phone from him? He couldn't even rationalise that it might be for business because if that was the case, he would have taken the phone to Paris with him. Did Khalid have a secret lover that he was keeping from James? His head pounded as he wondered what to do.

James' anxiety grew as he heard every sound and jumped. He paced the room back and forth as he considered his next move. After making copies of the documents he didn't understand, he carefully placed everything back as near as possible as it had been, apart from the phone. He clung onto that. The screen was dead, but he had a charger that he could use. He knew he would get in a lot of trouble with Khalid over this, but he couldn't help himself from pursuing his fears.

He left the phone charging, while he went online to look for an Arabic translator. Within an hour, he had read through all Khalid's documents and nothing seemed ominous or of any significance. Maybe the drawer was locked in innocence and there was no need for concern but the perspiration on James' brow said otherwise.

After checking the documents, he searched the net to find out how to get into Khalid's spare phone. James discovered there was spy software available to monitor the phone's activity, including finding out who was in the contacts and tracking the call logs and messages. James swallowed hard. This could mean the end of their relationship if Khalid found out James was checking up on him. For his peace of mind, he had to know, so he ordered the device.

The software arrived and after three hours of trial and error guessing passwords and usernames, James was about to give up. Suddenly, he remembered a box where Khalid put special things. James opened it and moved aside the ring he gave Khalid. There was a sheet of paper that he unfolded. His heartbeat increased. The document had Khalid's passwords on. After his eureka moment he was able to get into the phone's settings. This meant now he could monitor the phone's activity without any detection. He placed the phone back where he found it and came up with a cock and bull story. When Khalid returned, he had his explanation in place for why the drawer had been tampered with.

"I'm so sorry, Khalid. My laptop crashed, so I came in here to see if yours worked. I spilt coffee on the top of the table. Unfortunately, I could see that coffee had seeped into the drawer. I was worried that you may have important documents that could be ruined if I didn't dry them out." Just for authenticity, James had dabbed some coffee over the top few sheets of paper in the drawer.

Khalid didn't look too convinced. His eyes narrowed. Other than the phone, he had nothing to hide though. The phone was still in place. He wasn't happy but didn't want to make too big a deal out of it. He was tired after his trip.

James didn't have time to monitor the information he extrapolated from the phone until later the following day. It was the call monitor list that made his head reel. He looked at a phone number that kept cropping up. Why had Khalid been phoning James' father?

## Chapter 30

James lay awake the next night thinking over everything. He turned to look at Khalid deep in sleep. Did he really know his lover? He had a dilemma. If he challenged Khalid, he would have to reveal how he found out. The only solution was to speak to the man who had disowned him, the patriarch who had cast him aside and hadn't spoken to him for over five years. Challenging his father about his conversations with Khalid wasn't going to be easy.

After discussing the issue with Kylie and Dotty, he decided to tackle his mother first. He would see if she could throw any light on why Khalid and his father had been in contact with each other. James met his mother, Marjorie for coffee. She wasn't as keen as James to get to the bottom of the matter.

"Is it important why they spoke? You know what your father is like. He is unlikely to tell you, anyway. If everything is good between you and Khalid, then why spoil things. Can't you leave matters alone? You don't want to ruffle anyone's feathers." Marjorie's placid approach and calm nature was the only reason she'd been able to stay married to Ned for all these years. She kept out of his business life and was happy to spend his money. Where it came from or how he acquired it was of no interest to her. She had learnt long ago not to tackle Ned. Her motto was — anything for a quiet life. She felt her son should have the same approach.

"I don't know, Mother. I don't like it. Especially after what happened to the man who died, Mohamed Al Khalifa."

"Yes, but if you pursue this, it could blow up in your face and you could end up losing that lovely home of yours."

"I understand that, Mother, but there is more at stake here than money. I have a right to know what is going on."

"Could he have been in touch with your father to ask for your hand in marriage?"

"I doubt it. Khalid isn't going to marry me. He would never disrespect his family and marry someone of another faith, however much he may want to. He has told me that it would not be possible. No, I'm sure it can't be that."

"You know the saying that curiosity killed the cat. Be careful it doesn't harm you, dear."

They kissed as they left the coffee shop and went their separate ways. James felt no further forward but by the next day, he had come up with a plan.

"I'm going to go over to the farm to see my father and drop in unannounced. After all this time not seeing me, he may be pleased with me getting in touch. I will find out what is going on and why he and Khalid have contacted each other. After the last time I spoke to my father, I'm surprised he would entertain Khalid, so something has shifted. I'm sure it can't do any harm." Kylie and Dotty looked at each other with raised eyebrows.

"Well, if you're going, then I'm coming too. I don't want you getting hurt. If your dad is horrible to you, he's less likely to treat you badly in company." Kylie squeezed James' arm.

"Count me in as well," Dotty said. "I intended taking Winnie over there to have a snoop around anyway. Your two pairs of eyes are probably more use than Winnie's."

"You mustn't get involved."

"We insist," the girls chorused.

They arranged to go to Devil's Bridge Farm the following evening.

Kylie was glad to do something to take her mind off their up-and-coming exams. She was also glad to get away from Will. A rift had developed between her and her lover and she found it difficult to concentrate on her college work. They had been arguing again and if she mentioned the farm, it was like saying a swear word.

"Look, I don't get involved with your work, so why do you have to push your nose into my business." Will was not a happy bunny. He would be even more unhappy if he knew what Kylie had planned. The course of true love wasn't running smoothly at the moment for Kylie. She hoped being with Dotty and James would ease her worries.

James picked the two girls up that evening. They approached the main gate to the farm. James had second thoughts about entering.

"I don't know if this was such a good idea. My father knows what vehicle I drive. If he sees my car, he may not open the door."

"Okay, I've got a plan," Dotty said.

"What's that then?"

"We'll leave the car at the end of the lane and walk up. Kylie and I will go first, and you can bring up the rear, keeping out of sight. Once the front door is answered, you make your move and lurch forward. By springing a surprise on him, you'll hopefully gain entrance."

"Okay, I'll go along with that." James switched his engine off and left the car on the country lane. They scuttled up the tree-laden path like members of the SAS. They treated it like a military operation the way they ran to each tree then checked to see the coast was clear.

"Wait a minute, don't move forward yet. Someone's coming," Kylie called out. They heard the roar of a car engine. The sound got louder and closer. They crouched behind a bush and watched. Two men parked up and got out of a Range Rover. One had a beard and a bald head, the other wore a baseball cap brought down low that hid his features. Dotty and the others peeped through the trees and saw them lift the boot lid and take out several travel cages. They heard barking.

"I wish I had my binoculars to get a closer look."

Dotty nodded. They waited and watched as the two men took the animals around the back of the farm out of sight.

"What do you want to do, James? If your dad's got company, it might not be the best time to approach him."

"Shall we stay and see if we can find out what is going on here?"

"Yes, did you notice those dogs looked like pit bull terriers? I thought they were illegal," Kylie said.

"They are," James added as he got up off his hands and knees and dusted himself down. "Come on, let's get nearer. Keep out of sight. I want to see what those two are up to."

"Don't get too close. Those dogs looked vicious. Did you see that one of them had torn open the bars on its cage?" Dotty put an arm up to stop the other two passing. Slowly and stealthily, the three friends sneaked around the side of the building and followed the noise of the dogs barking. Some way ahead, they saw a section of the field had been mapped out with a wire pen. Two dogs were in the centre and being taunted to attack each other. The two men laughed and cheered.

The girls and James heard more voices.

"Ssh," James said, putting his finger over his lips. They watched as two more men joined the others. What they witnessed next was barbaric. At the first sign of blood, Dotty grimaced. She put her hands over her eyes. It was like watching a horror movie.

"I can't stomach any more of this. Those dogs are being trained to attack each other. Let's get out of here."

"Yes, I've seen enough. This has made me feel sick." James heaved.

"Wait a minute, there's someone else coming." Kylie stopped the others moving forward. They all bent down again.

"Oh no, have you seen who it is?" Dotty whispered, worried about being seen or heard.

"I don't believe it," Kylie added.

## Chapter 31

The person coming into view went up to the men, laughing and joking. He turned around. It was Will. Dotty looked across at her friend, her head cocked.

"What shall we do?"

"Those guys look as mean as the dogs. Let's get out of here."

The sight they had seen left the three friends shaken. They drove to the pub to discuss their findings. Kylie ordered herself a pint. She was still trying to process what she had witnessed.

"Are you going to tackle Will about it?" Dotty asked.

"Darn right I am. We thought Ned was farming puppies illegally, but dog fighting takes this to a whole new level." Kylie glugged her drink.

"What we saw proves my father is still the same as ever. The man has no scruples. He is just after making a profit whatever way he can. He disgusts me. I wish now I'd not got involved. We should have stayed at home revising for our exams."

"Oh, don't remind me. I'm dreading them." Dotty put her drink down and wiped around her mouth.

"Do you think your dad is in on the dogfighting?" Kylie asked.

"I'm sure he is. It's his land. That didn't look like the first time those guys had been there. A pen was set up in the field for the fight."

"The way those dogs set about each other was ferocious. How can anyone bear to watch something like that?" Dotty put her glass on the table.

"It's a sport to them. There will be arranged matches, you can bet, where more unscrupulous people put money on which dog they think will win." James took a sip from his glass of wine.

"Thinking about it, those times in the past when we've seen a convoy of cars arriving at the farm, that could be the reason. They may have been punters arriving to watch a match."

"You're right, it's disgusting. What can we do about it?" James didn't look happy.

"Would Khalid get involved in this?" Dotty asked. James shuddered,

"I doubt it. He hates cruelty to animals as much as I do."

"We need to catch them in the act. If we report it, it wouldn't take long for those guys to cover their tracks. They'll be wise to the authorities who may snoop around. We should think carefully about how we move forward with this."

"You're right. If we go to the police or the RSPCA, they may investigate but find no evidence. The best way would be to find out when a match is taking place and catch them then. We could video what we see but how can we do that?" Dotty looked across at the other two.

"I've an idea," Kylie said. "I could use my charm on Will to discover if there's a match coming up locally."

"He's hardly likely to talk." James frowned.

"Maybe not, but I'm good at plying him with drink and if I tell him what I know, I could mention I saw him there. He can't deny his involvement then."

"If you're sure you think it's a good idea."

Kylie did think it was a good idea and arranged to see Will that night. She should have been doing last-minute revising for her exams, but any excuse to get out of doing work suited Kylie. She would much prefer using her charms on her boyfriend to find out what was going on at the farm. Deep down, she hoped to talk him out of working there before things got worse. There must be plenty of farmhand jobs in the area. She invited him over to her place and she made up some cocktails and laced the red wine with brandy and vodka. She put on some slow seductive music and a low-cut dress. Will was impressed when he saw her.

"What's this? Is it my birthday or something?"

"Come and sit down, gorgeous. I'll fix you a drink."

"What's in it? It's strong." He shook his head as he took a swig from the glass that Kylie poured for him. She had set the room up with lights dimmed and candles burning.

"Get it down you. It's one of my specials." Kylie had a glass of red wine for herself. She hadn't added any spirits to hers, but Will didn't know that. "It's good, isn't it?"

"Are you trying to get me drunk?"

"No, not at all. I want you to have a good time while you're here. I know things haven't been so good between us lately, so I wanted to show my appreciation for having you in my life." Kylie came over and started massaging Will's shoulders. He put his hand around her neck and tried to kiss her.

"Wait, not so fast. That's for dessert. We've got a nice chicken pasta dish I've made." Kylie didn't give Will as large a portion as usual. She didn't want the food to soak up the booze. She wanted his tongue to be loose and talking freely. His cheeks glowed as the alcohol took effect, so she needn't have worried. They finished their food and moved to the sofa. Kylie started questioning Will. By then his eyes were glazed.

"I don't know what you put in that drink, but my head's gone woozy."

"You lightweight. I thought you were a man and could take your drink." Kylie smiled.

"I'm more of a man than anyone you've had before." Will moved to grab hold of Kylie but she moved away. "What's wrong?"

"You're so much of a man that you watch dogs tearing pieces out of each other, do you?" The smile disappeared off both Kylie's and Will's faces.

"What are you talking about?"

"I watched you at the farm with those guys and the pit bull terriers setting about each other. It was gruesome."

"I don't know what you mean."

"Don't give me that. You can't deny it, Will. The cat is out of the bag. I saw you."

Will leaned forward and put his head in his hands. He shook his head and thought for a few moments.

"You say you saw the dogs fighting. When was this?"

"It doesn't matter. The point is, that sort of thing is illegal, and you should seriously think about changing jobs. Ned Bristow is a wrong 'un."

"Who else saw it?"

"What do you mean?"

"Who was with you?"

"No one." Kylie didn't like how Will's eyes looked menacingly at her. She wouldn't implicate her friends as well.

"So, what were you doing there?"

"I'd gone to speak to Ned Bristow about the puppy farming."

"I told you to keep your nose out. Now, look what you've gone and done."

"Surely, you can't condone that sort of behaviour."

"I get paid well and don't ask any questions."

"But it's against the law."

"And have you never broken the law?" He laughed but his eyes narrowed. "I'm just doing my job. Those dogs were in training for a big match on Friday night. There's a lot of money riding on this one. It's a local championship."

"Really? That's interesting."

"Kylie, you can't tell anyone about this."

"People have a right to know."

"Kylie, whatever you think, you're not going to put a stop to it. It's too big a deal. Lots of wealthy men put money Ned's way over this."

"I'll do what I want. I'm sick of you trying to bully me." She gave him a shove and his drink spilt.

Will saw red. He grabbed hold of her and had his hands around her neck.

"Get off me. I don't answer to you." She tried to shake him off, pushing him again. This only made his anger worse. He went to punch her, but she anticipated the move and ducked. She got up off the sofa but wasn't quick enough and Will grabbed her. "How dare you hit a woman. I always knew you weren't a real man." She went to kick him, but he caught her leg. The comment had riled Will. If Kylie wasn't going to behave like a woman, then he wouldn't treat her like one. He moved in for the attack. He lashed out with punches and kicks. His larger frame soon overpowered Kylie. She was at his mercy.

# Chapter 32

The morning rain splattered against the kitchen windowpane as Dotty poured her cereal into a bowl. She felt a mixture of emotions as she walked towards the fridge and took out the milk. Her body tingled in anticipation of the day ahead. She opened her file out onto the table and started to read through her revision notes. As she mulled everything over in her head, she wished now she'd done more revising. Dotty went to pieces when it came to exams. She wasn't the sort of person who could stay focused long enough to concentrate on the job in hand. Today was no exception.

Yes, she was sitting her theory exam for hairdressing, but she had other things on her mind. The pressure was on. If she did badly today, she may not be allowed to continue on the course. The real stuff she was interested in was the beauty side of the business. Then there was Robin. They had spoken every day since Joe's twenty-first and even though they weren't physically together, she was developing strong feelings for him. He was constantly in her thoughts. They had so much in common. He loved fashion and history. He specifically loved all things relating to the Second World War which was an era that Dotty was so fond of learning about. They chatted for hours about memories that had been passed onto them by their grandparents, from the blitz to rationing. Dotty's gran had been a land army girl, so Dotty loved recounting the tales she had been told.

Robin was coming to see her the following weekend and Dotty couldn't wait. It had been organised for him to stay with Kylie. Dotty was grateful for her offering to put him up. Thinking about Kylie, Dotty was surprised that she hadn't been in touch to tell her how she went on with Will the previous night. Dotty had sent her a couple of text messages, but Kylie hadn't got back to her yet. Dotty assumed she had got Will drunk and probably had too much herself and was now in some boozed-up coma. Dotty didn't want to let the irritation she felt towards her friend fester, so instead, she read through the section on hair again.

*Hair is made up of a protein called keratin amongst other substances. The strands grow from an organ under the skin called a follicle which is found in the dermis of the skin, the deeper level. This area is the living part of the hair fibre.*

Dotty re-read the passage twice, but it wasn't going in. She sighed and closed her book. She sent another text to Kylie to see if she wanted to get to college early to test each other before their exam. She thought if they asked each other questions, the information may stick better. That plan went out of the window. There was still no reply from Kylie. Dotty decided to go in, anyway. She was too nervous sitting around at home. She preferred to be around others in the same position as her.

"Good luck, Dotty," her dad called out as she left the house.

"Thanks, Dad, see you later." She slammed the door shut and checked her phone. There was still no news from Kylie.

When she arrived at college, a few others had the same idea as her and they sat in the refectory churning over their notes going over the subject matter. Dotty sought out James to ask if he had heard from Kylie. She bumped into him by the lockers.

"James, how are you feeling about today?"

"Nervous but I should be okay. How about you?"

"I'm not as confident as you. Have you heard anything from Kylie?"

"No, I messaged her earlier, but she hasn't replied. That's not like her. She's usually on the ball."

"Maybe her phone died, and she's lost her charger or perhaps they ended up going out last night and she's lost it completely. You know what she's like when she's had a few. She's always losing things."

"Yes, that's probably it."

"She was intending to tackle Will about the dogfighting. I'm dying to know what he had to say about it."

"Yes, thinking about what we saw turns me cold." The pair looked up as they heard footsteps walking towards them. Rose came up to ask Dotty if she had a spare pen.

"Typical. I normally bring my pencil case full of them, but I forgot it with my nerves and everything. I've only got one pen, and that's packed in."

"You can borrow one of mine. I don't know why you're worrying." Dotty turned towards James. "Rose is excellent at everything, James. She's the teacher's pet."

"No, I'm not." They chatted and asked each other questions. Dotty kept one eye on the clock and another on the phone. There was still no word from Kylie. Time passed, and they were due in the exam.

They lined up outside the hall. By now, Dotty was really concerned about her friend. Even if she had a hangover, Kylie would pull out all the stops to get there. She was a trouper like that. She usually bounced back to life however much she's had to drink the previous evening. Kylie would come to and be as bright-eyed and bushy-tailed as the next person.

"Where is she?" Dotty whispered to James.

"Have you got Will's number? See if he knows where she is."

"Good idea." Dotty held back as the students filed into the hall. Her fingers and thumbs typed away.

"Switch that off, Dotty. You know phones aren't allowed in the hall." Her tutor frowned and her eyes narrowed.

"Yes, sorry."

"Is everything okay, Dotty?" The tutor noticed Dotty's complexion had turned pale.

"Yes, it's nerves. I'll be okay once this is all over."

"Go and take your seat. Did you bring some water?"

"Yes, I'll be fine, thanks."

Dotty found the desk that had her name on it and sat down. She felt nauseous. She checked Kylie's seat. The place was empty.

She turned back to look at James and mouthed, "Where is she?" He shrugged his shoulders and put his palms up to the ceiling. There was no sign of Kylie. She was going to miss her exam.

## Chapter 33

The students milled around in the corridor after the exam finished. They were busy comparing notes on their answers to the questions. Dotty wasn't interested. The knot in her stomach wasn't caused by wondering how she may have done. She was worried about her friend. Kylie hadn't shown up, late or otherwise. Something was wrong. Dotty could feel it in her bones. She walked along the corridor. The echo of her feet sounded against the laminate flooring. Rushing past the classrooms, she wondered what would happen to Kylie now she had missed the exam. It wasn't like her friend to be unreliable.

"Tut, tut, trust that mate of yours not to turn up for an important exam," Becky said. "She's not very reliable, is she?" Dotty ignored the remark and brushed past her. She walked up to the admin office and knocked on the hatch.

"Has Kylie been in touch?" she asked the middle-aged clerk. The woman shook her head.

"It doesn't look like it unless she spoke to her tutor directly." Dotty went in search of Paula Ridgeway, Kylie's form tutor. She walked back towards the hall and found her stood chatting with a huddle of students around her. Dotty eavesdropped on their conversations.

"You've done your best. That's all you can hope for. I wouldn't worry about it now the horse has bolted. There's no use crying over spilt milk if you got a question wrong." Dotty hovered on the edge of the group. Paula looked up. "Are you waiting for me?"

"Yes, I wondered if you had heard from Kylie. I've checked with the office and she didn't ring in there."

"No, it's a bit of a poor show. All that work has been wasted."

"Well, it won't have been…" Dotty watched as Paula turned her back to her. She was already talking to someone else before Dotty had time to reply. That was how concerned her tutor was about Kylie. Dotty sighed and went in search of James. She tried Kylie's phone again, but it went straight to answerphone. She left a message, unsure why she was wasting her time as none of the other messages had been answered. James was in the refectory having a coffee.

"James, any news?"

"No, I've not heard from her. I take it that you've not either?"

"No, and I'm getting concerned now." She wondered whether she should tell James she had a bad feeling about Will. She didn't like Kylie's boyfriend much, but, so far, had kept her opinions to herself. She bit her lip.

"What shall we do?" he asked.

"I'm going over to her flat to see if she's there. You never know, she may be ill in bed and slept through the exam."

"Let's hope that's all it is. While you're gone, I'll phone around her other friends and family that I know of. I have a few numbers I can check with. Any reply from Will?"

"No, I don't like it, James." Dotty shook her head. "Keep in touch."

Dotty's head was buzzing as she travelled over to Kylie's place. All manner of weird and wonderful scenarios went through her head where Kylie could be. She tried to be positive and imagined Will had won the lottery and whisked her off for a lavish last-minute holiday. Deep down though, she couldn't avoid thinking of the worst-case scenario — that something untoward had happened to her friend. When she arrived at Kylie's flat, she wasn't hopeful that she'd find her there. She pressed the buzzer and waited. Nothing. She tried again, tapping her feet on the ground, wondering what her next move should be.

Suddenly the outer door burst open and an elderly grey-haired lady pushing a shopping trolley appeared.

"Hello, Mrs Carmichael. How are you?" Mrs Carmichael lived in the flat next door to Kylie and constantly complained about the noises coming from Kylie's flat.

"I'm not too bad. It's a shame to go out in this though. It's blustery today, isn't it?"

"Yes, you be careful. The winds are so strong, they could knock you over."

"That's why I've got Sharon with me."

"Sharon?"

"Yes, dear, Sharon shopping trolley. That's what I've christened her. I have to have someone to talk to at nights when I'm feeling lonely. We discuss what I'm going to have for my evening meal. We have some good conversations. She never gets on my nerves. I might get on hers a bit, but she never says anything." Dotty laughed as she held the door open, so Mrs Carmichael could manoeuvre around the heavy outer door. She brushed past Dotty then turned and straightened her back. "What are you doing here, Dotty?"

"I came to see if Kylie was in but there's no answer. Do you know if anyone has a spare key for her place?"

"Mabel at number forty-two might. She's always in, so she takes Kylie's parcels in and things like that. I'm sure she had a key once to let the painter in. Check with her."

"Thanks, I will." She started to toddle off then stopped again.

"Won't she be at college?"

"No, she's not there. I've just come from an exam. Kylie should have been sitting it with me."

"Oh dear, she must have got cold feet."

"Yes." Dotty sighed and frowned.

Then as an afterthought, Mrs Carmichael added, "You know, I must have another word with her next time I see her. She and her boyfriend made a right din last night."

"Really, did you hear what they said?"

"No, but it sounded like they were arguing, and I heard crashing noises."

"Right." Dotty filled her cheeks and blew air out through her mouth. She didn't like the sound of this. She made her way to number forty-two. Thankfully, Mabel was in and had a key to Kylie's place. She wouldn't release it to Dotty, but she offered to go with her to let her in when Dotty expressed her concerns for her friend. Mabel waited in the doorway with her arms folded while Dotty checked for any signs of Kylie.

Dotty gasped when she viewed the mess in front of her.

"You better come in, Mabel."

"What's been going on here, then?" Mabel moved her hands to her hips.

"I don't know, but I don't like it."

There was a chair upturned, and cushions on the floor scattered about. A vase was smashed in the corner with a water patch on the carpet. Dotty ran through to check if Kylie was in any of the rooms.

"Kylie," she called out. "Are you there?"

Dotty was met with silence. She came back into the lounge and started to pick up the pieces of the broken vase when a thought struck her. Could this be a crime scene? Should she leave everything alone? She shuddered.

By now, Mabel had also started snooping around.

"Have you seen that on the wall by the dining table?"

"What's that, Mabel?"

"Those dark red splattered patches. Do you think it's wine or tomato sauce, maybe?"

Dotty walked forward and joined her. Together they peered towards the wall to inspect it more closely. The hairs on the back of Dotty's neck pricked. Both women looked at each other.

"Are you thinking what I'm thinking?" they both nodded. Dotty's stomach lurched.

"That's blood." She bit her lip.

## Chapter 34

Dotty phoned Dave. She should probably have dialled 999, but she needed to hear a friendly voice, hopefully, someone who would reassure her that she was imagining things and that all was well.

"It doesn't sound good," he said down the other end of the phone. "Are you sure it's blood?"

"We think so. It may have been there some time but the fact I can't get hold of Kylie makes it look more suspicious and I'm deeply worried."

"Stay there, I'll be right over. I was about to message you, anyway. I've got a copy of the photographs the witness took from the scene of Candice's accident. I want you to look at them to see if it jolts your memory in any way."

"Scan them in and send them over by email, if you can. I'll check them out while I wait for you." The pictures pinged through almost immediately. Dotty looked at the people in the crowd by the shopping mall. There was a man at the back that Dotty recognised but she couldn't think where from. She frowned.

Dave and another detective were soon there with them.

"I picked up some broken glass. I realise this could be a crime scene, so I didn't want to touch anything else." Dotty's expression was grave.

Dotty and Mabel were shepherded into Mabel's flat so that if forensics needed to get involved, there would be no further contamination by them.

"Have you any ideas where Kylie might be?" Dave asked Dotty.

"No, I've been in touch with James who phoned round her other friends and family. No one has seen or heard from her."

"Anything on the photos I sent?"

"No, but there was a guy on one I'm sure I know but I can't think where from."

"If anything comes to you, let me know." Dave nodded. He was about to speak when a police constable arrived in the doorway.

"Sarge, have you got a minute?"

Dave went over to talk to him. They spoke in low voices in the hallway. Dotty couldn't hear what they said. Dave's face looked bleak. He clasped his hands behind his back.

"What's the matter?" Dotty asked,

"We've retrieved Kylie's handbag from the bedroom. Her phone was in there. Do you think she would have gone out without taking her purse and phone with her?"

"No, definitely not." Dotty put her hand over her mouth and gulped.

"Then it's beginning to look like she's been abducted. Forensics are on their way."

Dotty rubbed the back of her neck. She paced up and down the room.

"Where can she be? What has he done with her?"

"Sit down, Dotty. We will find her."

"But you don't know that, and I feel like it's all my fault. I should have anticipated this and been here when she tackled Will." She raised her arms in the air in exasperation.

"You can't know everything. She could be with one of her friends and it may be all innocent.

Don't go jumping to conclusions." Dotty scowled at Dave. She stood up, crossed her arms, and stomped towards the window.

"Calm down, Dotty. It won't do the situation any good getting in a state."

Mrs Carmichael disturbed them bringing in a tray of drinks.

"Here, have a nice cup of tea to settle your nerves."

Dotty's hands shook as she lifted her saucer. The cup containing the hot tea rattled. She put it down again.

"I feel to blame. I never liked Will anyway. I should have realised he would do something like this."

"You can't predict someone's behaviour. You've done all you can by giving us a list of her friends. Now I'm needed next door. Are you going to be okay?"

"Yes, and if I think of anything else, I'll let you know."

"It goes without saying but stay out of it now. Let the police do their job."

"I can't just sit here doing nothing. I need to go and look for her."

"Dotty, I'm warning you. Stay away." Dave looked cross but as soon as he disappeared, Dotty finished her drink and she was off. There was no way she could sit about doing nothing. Her only consolation was there wasn't much blood, so, hopefully, nothing too serious had happened to Kylie. She hoped she could find her friend alive and she knew exactly where she was heading.

She drove like a maniac up to Devil's Bridge Farm. Lewis Hamilton would have been proud of the way she manoeuvred the corners along the narrow country lanes. She took a chance motoring around the blind bends, but her thoughts were on Kylie and what may have happened. She would never forgive herself if something bad had occurred.

With little thought for her own safety, she drove through the farmyard gate and marched up to the front door of the farm. She knocked on the door and waited. There was no answer. She stood looking around, hands on hips There had to be someone here. Where was everyone? She rushed back out towards the outhouses. She could hear the dogs barking but then she also thought she heard raised voices coming from inside one of the barns.

She ran up to it and slowly tried to turn the door handle, but it was locked tight. She checked again. There were definitely muffled sounds coming from inside. The sides of the building were made of corrugated iron. She looked up. There was a window in the roof. It was a single-storey building, so she wondered if there was any way she could get up there to hear what was going on inside.

She walked around the periphery of the building. She was in luck. A ladder was leant up the far side. She took it and carefully placed it close to the open window. Although she wasn't afraid of heights, she could have done without climbing up. She had done something similar once before when she forgot her keys at school and managed to climb in through her bedroom window. With that memory coming to the forefront of her mind, she knew she could tackle this move successfully. Unable to come up with a suitable alternative she started ascending the rungs of the ladder.

Dotty climbed onto the ridge at the corner of the building and slowly eased her way around to the window. She moved in towards it. Her eyes opened wide when she saw who was inside. Ned, Will and the man from the photograph that Dave sent her. Not only that, it suddenly came to her who he was — it was Bert. Mo, the cleaner's husband. Before Dotty left that job, Mo never stopped talking about him. One minute she was singing his praises, the next she was moaning about him. She had shown Dotty a photo of them both together. Looking down inside the barn, she double-checked. It was definitely Bert. She gulped as she took in this revelation. She couldn't afford to be seen but had to know what was going on. She leant forward to listen. The voices were low but when Dotty put her ear to the open window, she could hear what was being said.

"You're an idiot, Will. What possessed you to involve yourself with this cretin of a woman?"

"I didn't know she would be such a nosey cow and want to poke her nose into everything."

"Well, we need to get rid of her somehow before she comes round. We'll make it look like an accident just as we did with the Arab and that other woman. Trust you to get the wrong woman, Bert. If you had a brain, you'd be dangerous. Now we'll have to plan how to see her off properly this time."

Dotty's heart was going ten to the dozen. She couldn't believe what she had heard. Suddenly, the sound of a car engine driving towards the farm disturbed her. As she looked up, she lost concentration and her foot slipped and got caught in the edge of the window. She put her arm out but missed the corner of the frame. Unable to steady herself, she swerved forward. As she put her arms out, she fell, crashing through the window onto the ground inside the building.

Shards of glass surrounded her. Her ankle throbbed with pain but otherwise, she survived the fall. She brushed the glass away but couldn't move. Slowly, she looked up.

"Well, well, well, look who's dropped in. If it isn't the other meddlesome bitch."

Dotty's face grimaced. The severity of the pain was so intense. It took her a few moments before she noticed Kylie lying comatose in the corner by several bales of hay.

"Get up." Ned sneered then kicked her.

"I can't." She held onto her ankle, close to tears. A lightbulb went on in Ned's brain.

"Oh dear, that's a shame. You can't move, can you not? I've got an idea, Will. Do you have a light?"

Will threw a lighter to Ned who proceeded to walk over to one of the bales and set it alight.

"Come on, let's get out of here, lads." Ned, Will and Bert rushed out of the building.

At first, the fire smouldered, but it didn't take long before flames were licking the sides of the sturdy posts keeping the building erect. The sounds were like an orchestra tuning up, with gentle crackling followed by an almighty whoosh.

Under normal circumstances, Dotty would have lay there and waited for help or at least until the pain in her ankle subsided but this was no ordinary situation. With all her courage and might, she lifted herself off the ground. She hopped to her feet and hobbled over to where Kylie lay motionless. The degree of pain she was in was crippling. She fought back tears as she tried to wake her friend. It was useless. Kylie was unconscious and Dotty couldn't rouse her.

It wasn't the flames that were Dotty's main concern as much as the smoke. Thick grey clouds were already billowing around the building like hungry serpents. She put her arms around Kylie's arms and shoulders and dragged her towards the door. Unable to walk, she crashed to the ground with Kylie on top of her. This was hopeless. It was a real struggle but the sight of the flames getting ever closer meant she couldn't afford to give up. She balanced on one leg and pulled Kylie along, but it was virtually impossible. There was no time for niceties, so she got hold of Kylie's feet and dragged her over the concrete floor.

"Sorry, Kylie," she said. "I must get you out of here."

She collapsed with the weight of the body then raised herself up again on all fours. Coughing and spluttering, she continued with what seemed an enormous task. She used the corner of her jumper to place over her mouth. Her elation turned to panic as she reached the outer door of the building and realised it was locked. She called out for help, but the smoke became too much. Dotty choked on the fire clouds one last time before she passed out.

## Chapter 35

Fortunately for Dotty, the car she heard arriving that sent her spiralling down into the outhouse was the police. Dave and his colleague had already tried the main farmhouse and got no reply. It was then that Dave noticed smoke rising from the farmyard.

"Come on, mate. Let's get over there." Dave and PC Neil Gladstone rushed over towards the direction of the blaze. They tried the door of the building. It was locked but Dave gave an almighty kick with his size nines and managed to force it. They were met with the sight of Dotty and Kylie's bodies by the entrance. The police officers pulled out the two women just in time. Minutes later, there was a huge crashing sound and the whole building became an inferno and came tumbling to the ground.

Dave had alerted the rest of the emergency services who arrived in no time. A sooty faced Dotty woke up to see Dave and two dishy looking firemen peering down at her. She took the oxygen mask off her mouth briefly.

"What are you doing here?"

"I could say the same about you. It's a good job I arrived when I did. I got you out of there in the nick of time."

"I heard everything, Dave."

"Don't talk now. Let the paramedics look after you. We will take a statement later."

Dotty and Kylie were taken to hospital and were checked over. Amazingly, there was no serious smoke damage to their lungs. Dotty had broken her ankle, so she would be out of action for a while. They were both released that evening. Dotty's parents took them back to their house to give them both some TLC.

"I'll be indebted to Dave forever for saving us," Dotty said putting her foot up on the coffee table.

"I always said he was a good copper," Dotty's dad said. He brought in a hot drink for the girls.

"I know, we must take him out for a meal as a thank you. He saved our lives, as did you, Dotty. I don't know what would have happened if you hadn't arrived when you did." Kylie wiped back a tear. "I'm still coming to terms with what Will did to me. I really cared about him." Her face was a mass of cuts and bruises.

Just then the doorbell rang. It was Rachel. She'd come to see how the two wounded soldiers were doing.

"I'm relieved it's over and we got to the bottom of it. A police officer has been and taken a statement. They arrested those three scoundrels. After what I heard, I'll be a witness in the trials, but I can live with the ordeal if justice is to be done. Those men deserve to be put away for a long time."

"It was a mistake to go in alone looking for me, but I'm so glad you did, Dotty. I will never be able to repay you for finding me."

"You've both had a nasty ordeal and were lucky to get out of it alive. I don't know what I would have done if anything had happened to either of you." Rachel hugged her two friends.

"We need to get our lives back to normal now."

"What will happen over your missed exam, Kylie?" Rachel asked.

"I've spoken to the principal. She said that in view of the extenuating circumstances I can sit it first thing in the morning if I feel up to it."

"Oh, lucky you," Rachel said sarcastically. "That's all you need after what you've been through."

"To be honest, I'll be glad to take my mind off what happened and get it over with. I'm grateful that they're allowing me to sit the exam."

"Robin is coming down from Manchester later this week for a long weekend. Are you still okay to put him up, Kylie or do you need some time alone?"

"Of course, he can stay. No, I need my friends around me right now. I'm feeling vulnerable and weepy."

Rachel squeezed her friend's hand.

"You can come over to our place anytime you want if you can put up with our pesky parrot. Harry has trained her to say, 'pieces of eight' and it's so annoying. The bird keeps repeating it, over and over," Rachel said. Kylie laughed for the first time that day.

"Thanks, I may take you up on that offer and hopefully we can forget about those evil guys. I can't believe Ned tried to have me bumped off and Will was in on it."

"He says he didn't know that was Ned's intentions. It didn't take a rocket scientist to figure that Candice being pushed under that lorry was a case of mistaken identity."

"The judge and jury will decide their fate."

Dotty received a text from Robin saying he couldn't wait to see her and look after her. While Dotty was busy replying, the doorbell rang again. It was Dave. He came over and hugged her.

"I've finished my shift," he said. "I wanted to find out how you both were."

Dotty wiped a tear away.

"My eyes are still smarting, and my throat feels tight," Kylie said.

"Yes, and the smoke damage has left me with a headache, but I can live with that. I'm so glad to see you and I'm sorry for meddling."

"It's a good job I know you so well and guessed where you'd be. What am I going to do with you?" Dave shook his head.

"We're both so grateful to you and your colleague, Dave. I can never thank you enough." Kylie looked close to tears.

# Epilogue

Robin came down that weekend and Dotty spent most of the time at Kylie's flat. It was just what the doctor ordered for both girls. Dotty was pleased to have her new man around the place and Kylie was glad of the company. She didn't want to spend too long on her own reflecting on what could have been. She was here now and back in the moment and getting on with her life again. Kylie sat her exam and was grateful she had been given the opportunity. It obviously did Robin good as well being down south because he returned two weeks later and two weeks after that.

"This is becoming something of a habit, you coming to see me." Dotty smiled at him on his next visit.

"Yes, and it's getting expensive, all this petrol money to see you. I'll have to think of a way around it."

"I wish I could come up north and see you more but with college and work it's difficult."

"I understand."

Dotty lay awake at night wondering if Robin really did understand. She worried whether their long-distance relationship could last through the trials and tribulations of life. Poor Kylie was planning on steering clear of men since what happened with Will. She had lost trust in them. Poor James's relationship was rocky for a while. It turned out that Mohammed, the man trampled to death worked for Khalid. Khalid's motives were honourable though. He found out about the animal cruelty at the farm and wanted to put an end to it. The only way he could think to do that was to offer Ned money to stop his activities. Not only did Ned not take kindly to Khalid interfering, he decided to frighten off the man who came to the farm to offer him a bribe to stop the animal torture. Ned's greed was such that he was incensed by anyone interfering. His plan was to send out a warning for Khalid to keep away. He was able to cause the stampede by sending a dog into the cattle which freaked them out. He said he didn't intend for Mohammed to die. His intention was to warn him off and to stop Khalid meddling. Khalid had kept quiet about it because he thought James would leave him if he knew he had been interfering in his life. It had taken time for the lovers to patch things up. James was more upset with Khalid not saying anything to him.

"James, I promise I will never withhold information from you again. I love you and want to be with you." James sulked around for a while but eventually after a barrage of gifts and apologies, he made up with Khalid. The two weeks in Barbados helped them rekindle their relationship. James was going to need all the support he could to come to terms with his father going to prison. His mother had filed for divorce and was forcing Ned's arm to sell the farm. She wanted a fresh start and her son promised to help her. Hopefully, they would be a comfort for each other in the months ahead until everything died down and Ned was put away for life.

Robin came down for the trial to be there for Dotty when she gave evidence. The outcome was that Ned, Will and Bert were all given long sentences. Their detention also put a stop to any future dog fights.

"I can't believe you took a week off work to support me through this difficult time."

Dotty held onto Robin's hand.

"That's not the only reason for my visit."

"Oh?"

"No, there's something I need to tell you." That sounded ominous. Dotty didn't like conversations that began with that phrase.

"What is it, Robin?"

"You know how much I care about you, at least I hope you do." Dotty nodded. "And I think you feel the same way about me."

"Oh, I do, I do." She continued to nod and gripped his fingers.

"Well, I've come to a decision." He coughed and squirmed in his seat.

"What's that then, Robin?"

"If we're to take this relationship to the next level, we need to see more of each other."

"I know, but how is that possible? You know how busy we both are. I've got my studies on top of that…" Dotty was about to continue putting up an argument about how impossible their situation was. Robin put a hand over her mouth to stop her talking.

"I've come up with a solution. I've got an interview tomorrow with a large organisation close by. They need an electrician. If I get the job, I can move here, and we can get a place together."

"Really? You're serious about us?"

"Of course, I am, so I thought I'd better show you how much you mean to me by my actions."

"I can't believe you'd do that for me, sacrifice your friends and family up north to be here."

"Well, if that doesn't convince you I care, nothing will. I can't bear to be apart from you."

Dotty's heart melted. They kissed and held each other in a long embrace.

Robin went for his interview the following day and got the job. Dotty was ecstatic when he told her. Already she was planning where they could live and had started looking at places to rent.

"It's so exciting. I can't believe how much my life has changed. There's just one major concern I have that we need to discuss."

"Oh, and what's that then?" Robin took in a gulp of air and waited for the reply.

"Can I bring Winnie?"

Robin sighed. He frowned and his eyes narrowed. Dotty feared the worst.

"I'm not used to having animals around me."

"Please, Robin. She means the world to me."

Robin stared across at Dotty for a few moments. The anticipation and the silence were killing her.

"Of course, she can stay. I was only kidding."

"Oh, you," Dotty said, punching him playfully in the ribs.

# Reviews

If you enjoyed this book, I would really appreciate if you would leave a review.
Just a few short words on Amazon and maybe Goodreads and Bookbub would go a long way towards helping me.
Your encouragement helps stoke the fires of my creativity.

To improve my writing and to spur me on to write more, it is important that I get feedback from you, my readers.
Your opinion matters to me.
I greatly appreciate your time and effort.

# VIP Club Sign-up Reminder

**If you enjoy my writing and are interested in some of the other books I have written, you can sign up to my VIP club**

I am looking to build a relationship up with my readers, so I send out weekly newsletters to people who join my VIP club. These include otherwise untold information about the characters, things about me, and other bits of news including lots of freebies and offers.

I would love you to join and in return for giving me your email which will never be passed on to third parties, you will receive exciting goodies and give-aways not found anywhere else.

You can find the sign-up page on my website

**Website:** http://dezzardwriter.com/
**Email:** support@dezzardwriter.com
**Facebook:** https://www.facebook.com/dezzardwriter/
**Twitter:** https://twitter.com/diane_ezzard
**Bookbub:** http://bit.ly/2OlnLE1
**Amazon:** https://amzn.to/2Qf2uZV

# About the Author

Manchester born Diane Ezzard writes psychologically charged domestic noir mysteries and thrillers about ordinary people coping with extraordinary circumstances. She is the author of the Sophie Brown series. She previously worked as a HR manager, counsellor and managed a charity among other jobs.

She now lives and works in South-East England close to her daughter and young grandchildren where she spends her time writing when not fighting pirates and monsters.

# Acknowledgements

A big thank you goes to Samantha Ezzard for the great looking cover.
Thanks go especially to my team of readers and my fan base.
Without your praise and encouragement, I would not be spurred on to continue writing the way that I am.

Other Books by the Author

# Dotty Dices with Death
# Book 1 in the Dotty Drinkwater Mystery Series.

"Suspicious death of local DJ," read the headlines. The man of Dotty's dreams turns into something of a nightmare.

Meeting the tall, dark, handsome foreigner at her new job in the casino, Dotty thought all her Christmases had come at once. Instead, she discovers a trail of lies and deceit, to say nothing of a suspicious package.

Was Dotty the last one to see him alive? Do the police suspect she is involved?

With the help of her friends, Dotty sets out to unravel the mystery around the tragic murder before she gets locked up herself.

She should never have ignored the warning given by the mystery woman.


Available through Amazon

# Chapter 1

Dotty took off her fluffy olive-green beanie hat and scratched the top of her head. She made her way to the back of the bus and found an empty seat by the window. As CEO of her own company, it wasn't ideal travelling this way. It couldn't be helped, however, as her car had been making that funny noise again. She wouldn't put up with it any longer. After all, it might be something serious and she could hardly run her gardening business with no vehicle. So, she dropped it off at the garage first thing. It was handy that she had no customers booked in today other than a potential new client to visit. She'd look strange getting on the bus with a lawnmower and other gardening tools. What would her nosey neighbour, Betty Simpson think? There would be no end of moaning from Betty if she took up extra room with her equipment. Nudging Betty who sat on the seat in front, she smiled.

"Cold out, today," she said.

"Yes, dear. Where's your car?" Betty didn't miss a trick. She was the go-to person if you wanted to hear any gossip.

"It's in the garage for a service." That wasn't the whole truth but sometimes a little white lie was the easiest option with Betty. Dotty was in no mood for explaining irregular car noises this morning. Betty didn't need to know the ins and outs. She embroidered stories enough and came up with her own version, anyway. Knowing Betty, if she decided that Dotty's car had really been towed away for getting behind with the repayments, then that's what she would tell everyone. Betty could tarnish your name with her misrepresentations before you could click your fingers.

Dotty thought about changing her car for a van. It would be more practical, but it didn't go with her image and street cred. Besides, she was fed up of gardening. It was okay in the summer months when the weather was warmer but now the colder weather had set in, there wasn't as much to do, and it was freezing working outside. She'd not given that much thought when she was talked into starting up this little one-woman business by her two friends, Rachel and Kylie.

It was alright for them. They both had their nice warm jobs working inside. Rachel worked in an office and Kylie worked as a barmaid at Ye Olde Six Bells. Neither girl was happy in their jobs, but they weren't as miserable as Dotty. They always had a moan when the threesome met up on a Saturday. Although, if they all wanted to go on holiday together next year, they would have to grin and bear it.

Dotty wasn't on the bus for long. She checked the address beforehand and knew which stop to get off. If the Braithwaite's hadn't lived at the top of a hill, she'd have taken her pushbike, but it was too steep to tackle, and the forecast was for rain later. She shuddered and vowed to put some effort into looking for a new job. There had to be better ways than this to make a living. It could be worse. She could be in India working in the paddy fields or — no she couldn't think of any jobs worse than gardening right now. Even India would be warmer than Sussex. She looked out the window and watched a gust of wind pick up the leaves as they took flight through the air.

Dotty arrived at the location and jumped off the bus. She immediately felt the chill of the wind on her cheeks. She tossed her head back and walked up to the house. Her mind wandered as she thought about working in a bar in Ibiza or picking strawberries in Portugal, anything warm away from this biting cold weather. She looked up at the large house and groaned as she rang the doorbell. The door creaked open and the tall, pinched face of Mr Braithwaite stared down at her as she stood waiting on the bottom step.

"Oh, you're a girl. Well, I suppose its women's lib, and anything goes these days. You'd better come through." He walked in front and Dotty scurried behind. "It's a girl, Marjorie. It's a girl." Dotty thought it sounded like someone had just given birth.

"Yes, I know it is, Albert. Now run along and make yourself useful." Albert stood in the doorway frowning. "Make a drink." She shooed him out of the room. "Have a seat. Dotty, isn't it?"

Dotty nodded and plonked herself down on a grey corduroy sofa. The Braithwaite couple were retired, and Mrs Braithwaite had seen Dotty's card in the local hairdresser's shop. Albert returned not long after with a tray of drinks and a plate of chocolate digestives. Under normal circumstances, Dotty would refuse the biscuits as she was dieting again, but she took one to be polite.

"Take a few. We only get them in for guests. We both have diabetes and can't eat them." Dotty thought it strange to buy biscuits they couldn't eat, so she took another two to show her consideration and smiled. She finished her drink and Marjorie asked her all the questions she could think of. Marjorie wanted to know more about Dotty's family than finding out her prowess as a gardener. In fact, the only question relating to gardening was about her age.

"You look very young to have your own gardening business, dear."

"I'm twenty-seven."

"Gosh, you don't look that old." Dotty believed her youthful looks were more down to her beauty regime than her genes. She used a face pack twice a week, exfoliated on alternate days, always used serum and moisturiser and gave her face a deep cleanse every bedtime. She had also recently splashed out on eye cream and neck cream because you can't be too careful. Wrinkles could appear any time. With all the effort she put in, she hoped to still look youthful in her sixties and seventies if she could keep up her efforts until then.

"Thank you," Dotty said, blushing.

"So, you're not married, yet?" Marjorie asked as she pointed to Dotty's bare wedding ring finger.

"No, I'm very much single. My last relationship was a disaster. Ray was a nightmare to get rid of. He just wouldn't take no for an answer. We were only together for a short time and it's taken me months to get him to see I'm not interested."

"Oh dear, young love never runs smooth. Those were the days. I knew straightaway when I met my Albert that he was the one for me. You know immediately, don't you, dear?"

"I wish Ray could have worked out sooner he wasn't the one for me. He must have been thick not to get the message." Marjorie gave a shallow sigh. From her nostalgic gaze, she was no longer listening to Dotty. Her memory cells sprang forward with visions of Albert as a young man with his long hair. They were both teenagers in the Swinging Sixties but were more mod than rocker. Albert owned a gleaming blue scooter and would take Marjorie on day trips to Southend. Ah, those were the days.

"Would you like me to show you the work we want you to do?" Marjorie asked, coming back into the moment.

"Yes, of course."

"Follow me. There's a lot." Marjorie pulled a face. "Albert can't do it anymore with his bad back."

They walked around to the back of the house. Dotty was taken out to the garden.

"Wow, that's huge."

"Yes, it's rather deceptive. You can't tell from the front of the house just how much land is round the back. As you can see, we have a lot of trees which means a lot of leaves." Dotty had never seen as many leaves as those sat in the Braithwaite's' garden. It was as though they had been collecting them up for her. "Do you have one of those machines that hoover them up?"

"No, but I'm sure I can get hold of one." She stood admiring the hues of orange and brown that nature produced in autumn just before the harshness of winter took the last few leaves away. There were speckles of yellow and red to inspire her creative juices. As Dotty spoke, a gust of wind brought another ton of leaves swirling into the garden. She worried that as soon as one set of leaves cleared, another would appear. She'd have preferred to be out there painting the scenery rather than clearing it away.

The two women stood together viewing the spectacle for some time. More leaves fell from the interlocking branches of the trees above. This would be a thankless task. It wasn't a good idea to take this job on, but Dotty needed the money. She was at the stage of borrowing off her mum to go on a night out and that wasn't good.

They moved into the kitchen to discuss terms. Dotty didn't know how much hiring a leaf machine would set her back, so she added on extra to compensate. She showed Marjorie the price as she seemed to be in charge and the one holding the purse strings in this house. They had just shaken on the deal when a crashing sound came from the hall. Both women looked at each other with raised eyebrows.

"It's only me, Gran," came a voice that Dotty thought she recognised. She frowned and seconds later a tall young man stood at the kitchen door.

"Oh, it's you. What are you doing here?" he swept his lanky fringe off to the side.

"Hello, Ray. How are you?" Dotty had a sickly feeling growing inside her stomach.

"Do you two know each other?" Marjorie looked at them both.

# Book One in the Sophie Brown series –

## I KNOW YOUR EVERY MOVE

**A sinister phone call, an unknown visitor. Sophie's life is about to be turned upside down**

Sophie has worked hard to free herself from the clutches of addiction and turn her life around. Practising as a counsellor, in a women's centre in Manchester, she now helps other girls in trouble. She forms a close relationship with Cassie, one of her clients and tries to help her escape the clutches of a violent boyfriend.

But is Sophie being followed?

How can she uncover the truth, when she can't trust what is real?
The more she delves, the closer she gets to danger. Can she revisit her own dark past before it is too late?

Get hooked on this dark, twist-filled suspense thriller that's in the vein of works by Rachel Abbott and Mark Edwards.

                Available through Amazon -

## Chapter One

## YESTERDAY

Something soft and feathery brushed past the end of my nose. I sneezed and opened my eyes.

"Oh Max," I said.

The vision of loveliness that met me made me smile. What an adorable furry sight to wake up to in the morning. Sat on top of the silver satin duvet cover lay Max, the new addition to my family. At twelve-weeks-old, Max was a cute, mischievous bundle of joy. With big doleful eyes looking up at me, my heart melted. I stroked his velvety golden coat and tickled him under his chin.

"Want your breakfast, Max?"

I ignored the sound of him purring as I pressed my phone and looked at the time. 6.42. I groaned. I didn't need to get up early today. It was Saturday, so no work and I'd had a fitful night's sleep.

I'd had that dream again. The same one I'd been having over the last few months. I was running away from something or someone. I didn't know what, but I always woke up full of tension and fear. Thankfully, I never got caught. One minute I was jogging by the river, on my usual route, the next I'd been transported to a house. The combination of the red poppy wallpaper and mint green leather sofa was a scene I knew well from my childhood. Mum stood by the mirror in the hall, carefully putting on her lipstick. She wore the last outfit I'd seen her in, a tan polo neck ribbed jumper and fawn herringbone tweed skirt. I pulled at her arm.

"Please come, Mum." She didn't acknowledge me.

"Mum, come on, we need to go." No response.

"Hurry up Mum." Still, she ignored me.

I wasn't happy. Whether it was the bright shade of her crimson lip colour I didn't like or the fact she didn't respond to me, I didn't know.

In the dream, I began to panic as I sensed trouble brewing. I kept looking around. I had to act now. I tried one last time, shaking her.

"Mum, Mum, we've got to leave." She continued to face the mirror.

"Come on Mum, we've got to go."

I shouted out, but Mum still didn't acknowledge me. I began to cry. Fear enveloped me. I knew we were in danger. I watched her as she slowly applied another coat of lipstick and massaged her lips against each other. She didn't respond to me, so I turned away from her and ran.

That was when I woke up. Slowly, I re-entered the land of the living with a big stretch. Max jumped off the bed. My palms were sweating, and my pulse was racing. The anxiety rose in my chest. I had left Mum again and even though I knew it was only a dream, I didn't feel good. My stomach ached as I thought of the memories of her.

Might as well get up now I'm awake, I thought and walked over to open the curtains. I squinted as I looked outside. It wasn't the brightness of the day that greeted me. The clouds looked grey and forlorn. I begrudgingly put my dressing gown on and pottered into the kitchen.

I had Max now to look after, and I enjoyed spoiling him. My first job in a morning was to get him a saucer of milk and his food.

"Come on Max, here's your breakfast," I said. He didn't even give me the chance to get the food out of the can. He had his nose busy poking inside, trying to get at the fishy delights.

There weren't many places for a kitten to wander around and explore, especially with a flat as small as mine. When he got bigger, I knew I would have to let him out to discover the big wide world, and that scared me.

After feeding Max, I reached up into the cupboard to get the breakfast cereal. I sat for a few minutes, crunching a mouthful of fruit and fibre, contemplating the day ahead. Saturday usually meant doing chores which I detested, followed by a trip down to the shops to get my groceries for the weekend.

Shopping list done, I began milling around the place, starting with tidying up the kitchen. After walking into the hall to get the mop out of the cupboard, I checked myself out in the mirror.

My hair looked tangled, so I picked up the hairbrush and brushed it. It had a sheen and style that many women envied. I loved the comments I got about my beautiful long red locks.

The flat never seemed lonely on a Saturday, thanks to James Martin. Saturday Morning Kitchen was a favourite TV programme of mine. It formed part of my weekend ritual that included eating a bacon butty for lunch and a curry later that night. I didn't think of myself as a creature of habit, but there were certain behaviours that ran so deep, they were a regular part of my life now.

I had a passion for food, which spanned from cooking to watching cookery programmes on TV. I owned a vast range of recipe books and of course, I loved eating. Thankfully, I enjoyed running, as my frame would have been a lot larger had I not.

I wasn't one to try new recipes; I usually kept to classics like chilli and fish pie. I often dreamed of being the head chef of a Michelin-starred restaurant. Sadly, the culinary skills I possessed fell a long way short of that. Sometimes, I'd be in the shower, merrily singing away and realise that the sound accompanying me wasn't violins but the smoke detector going off in the other room. I would then remember that I'd put a couple of rashers of bacon under the grill.

I was concentrating on watching Rick Stein making a fish stew before getting up to tackle the ironing. Wrestling to put the ironing board up wasn't easy in the small confines of the kitchen. There was very little room to manoeuvre. I sighed heavily and frowned. I didn't like housework, least of all the ironing.

Suddenly the house phone rang. The old-fashioned cream coloured telephone sat a few feet from where I stood. I'd bought it to tone in with my muted decor. The penetrating sound of the intermittent bell ringing made me jump, and with jerked shoulders, I listened intently to the shrill tone. It was unusual to hear the house phone these days. Most people phoned me on my mobile. In fact, I only used the landline for the internet, so I couldn't imagine who it could be. Only Dad rang me on the landline, and we had a set time every Sunday night to speak. He never detracted from that, so I knew it couldn't be him. I decided not to answer. It was probably one of those PPI compensation calls or the ones that ask if you've been involved in an accident.

The phone got louder with every ring. The noise had distracted me from the ironing, and lacking concentration, I hadn't realised that I'd misjudged the iron plate. The hot iron toppled over, and I instinctively put my hand out to catch it.

Damn, I swore under my breath. The heat of the iron burnt through to my fingers and I screamed out. I was annoyed with myself for being so stupid. I quickly managed to shimmy past the ironing board to get to the sink. I put my hand under the cold-water tap. Ow, did that hurt. I kept my fingers under the icy blast of water, and I heard the phone still ringing.

That didn't sound like a friendly bell, more like the harsh warning sound of a siren. The loud noise blocked out the pleasant familiar tones of the omelette competition on TV. I urged the phone to stop. My heart pounded, and my fingers throbbed with pain. Why didn't it stop? I became irritated. The constant sound of the phone began to take on a macabre tone, and I became afraid to remove my hand from under the cold flow of water. Should I answer? No, I've left it this long.

My mind started playing tricks on me. Memories flooded back of a time when I had been trapped in the clutches of someone else's obsessions. A shudder came over me. What if it's him? No, I knew I was being silly now.

What if it's important? Pull yourself together, girl. If it's urgent, they'll leave a message, I told myself. I turned the tap off at the same time the phone stopped ringing. I picked up the remote control and turned off the TV.

The silence was eerie, and I could feel the thudding of my pulse. A knot churned over in my stomach and nausea crept up from my guts into my throat. My palms started to sweat, and the perspiration dripped from my forehead. My mouth was dry. A tightness developed in my chest and I bit my lip. Why was I getting so nervous about a phone ringing?

I walked over to the table, tentatively picking up the receiver with my good hand. My nerves erupted when I heard the tone that indicated there had been a message left. Stop getting so worked up, girl.

This was stupid. Breathing rapidly, I took the phone to my ear. A wave of cold air came over me as I listened intently. And I listened, and I listened. Nothing. I breathed a sigh of relief. Probably one of those nuisance companies, I thought.

I shook my throbbing hand and decided to leave the ironing until another time. I went into the bathroom to get a shower. I stood under the hot water for longer than normal and I chastised myself for getting so worked up over the phone. The water poured down, covering my body. The heat of it felt good. My fingers were still smarting. The shower door normally gave adequate sound proofing but, even with soap in my ears, I heard the ringtone of the house phone again.

I'll leave it, I thought to myself. It's probably the same annoying company that rung earlier. The ringing had stopped by the time I got out but, when I reached for the towel, it started up again. I was becoming irritated now.

Briskly drying myself down, I put on my dressing gown then went back into the kitchen to make myself a drink. I put the water in the kettle. The phone started ringing again. Whoever was phoning certainly wasn't taking no for an answer, so I decided to check the phone for messages in case an emergency had come up.

I knew I shouldn't be agitated over this, but I'd had such bad experiences in the past with menacing calls. I now had an unfounded fear around phones. Blind panic overwhelmed me as I listened and heard the distorted robot-like voice of a text call coming through the receiver.

"DON'T THINK YOU CAN GET AWAY WITH THIS."

What on earth did that mean? Get away with what? It was a strange message, and I didn't understand. Then I realised there was another message to listen to, so I pressed the button and waited.

In the same spooky, tinny voice of technology I heard, "SLUTS END UP GETTING WHAT THEY DESERVE." I started shaking.

I wondered if I could have misheard the messages so played them again. No, there was no mistaking the words. I pressed in the digits to find out the number the calls had been sent from, but the voice came back, 'Caller number withheld.'

I walked over to the sofa and sat down, my shoulders hunched, slowly taking in what had just happened. I wrapped my arms around my body and rocked from side to side, thinking. Was this a wrong number and all a mistake or could this be something more sinister?

# Bibliography

## The Sophie Brown Mystery Series –

### My Dark Decline – prequel

*One woman's journey from oblivion to recovery*

### I Know Your Every Move – Book 1

*A sinister phone call, an unknown visitor — is Sophie being followed?*

### As Sick As Our Secrets - Book 2

*Secrets and lies are rife in the dark world of gangsters and criminals.*

### The Sinister Gathering - Book 3

*Sophie went on a retreat hoping to find peace, instead, she found the body of a woman she had just met*

### Resentments and Revenge – Book 4

*A murdered young woman, a missing schoolboy, are they connected?*

### A Life Lost – Book 5

*She lost her memory and then her life.*

### The Killing Cult – Book 6

*Sophie makes a horrific discovery when she stumbles on a deadly cult.*

# The Dotty Drinkwater Mystery Series -

### Dotty Dishes the Dirt – prequel

*Dotty unearths more than she bargains for when she digs up human bones.*

### Dotty Dices with Death – Book 1

*The man of Dotty's dreams turns into a nightmare when he is found dead under suspicious circumstances.*

### Dotty Dreads a Disaster – Book 2

*That's not a pile of old clothes that Dotty discovers lying in the duckpond, it's a body.*

### Dotty Dabbles in Danger – Book 3

*Who is the mystery man that was trampled to death by cattle down at Devil's Bridge Farm?*

### Dotty Discovers Diamonds – Book 4

*The lavish birthday party turns to disaster when a man is found murdered.*

### Dotty Deals with a Dilemma – Book 5

*Find out what happens when Dotty's boss and her son disappear, and a ransom note comes in for them.*

Printed in Great Britain
by Amazon